Root Cause

A Collection of Stories on Community

Published by Inspired Quill: November 2025

First Edition

Content Warning: This work contains mentions of Assault, Gun Violence, Death (of family members), Sexism, Homelessness and War.

Please note that these stories have been edited in their original language. This means you may read "realized" in one story and "realised" in another, depending on where the author is from. Both are correct.

Chief Editors: E.A. Mylonas, Sara-Jayne Slack
Proofreader: Clare Stevens
Cover Design: Martina Pellecchia
Formatted By: BB eBooks Thailand
Typeset in Garamond

Paperback ISBN: 978-1-913117-39-9
eBook ISBN: 978-1-913117-40-5
Print Edition

1 2 3 4 5 6 7 8 9 10

Inspired Quill Publishing, UK
Business Reg. No. 7592847
www.inspired-quill.com

Foreword

Writing this foreword at a time when the news is full of watershed moments – moments made out of climate existentialism and political horror – was always going to be an interesting exercise.

This was never meant to be an "issues" anthology. From the start, the goal was to craft an offering to readers and, in the process, give some help to the communities that need it. What you're holding in your hands is a collection of short stories that celebrates community. Groups of people coming together for a common cause, despite their ideological, cultural, and other differences.

Let me backtrack here for a moment.

Let me tell you about meeting Sara-Jayne Slack.

Sara is the heart and soul behind Inspired Quill, the publisher of this book. It was during the time when we were discussing my first novel back in 2021, emails going back and forth, that she asked me to jump on a video call with her. What she wanted to find out was whether my own heart was in the right place.

See, Inspired Quill has, since its inception, funnelled profits into worthy causes. Books for underprivileged people, mentorships, supporting LGBT+ rights. It might not come as a surprise to you that not everyone appreciates this sort of work, but it definitely surprised me. Perhaps I was naive to think that an organization built on the principles of giving wouldn't attract any (mostly online) backlash. But perhaps this is symptomatic of all the division that spills out of our screens. Things weren't much better when we first had that discussion back in 2021, but in July 2025 it feels like something has fundamentally broken. In the US, in Europe, and elsewhere.

Was my heart in the right place? Was I willing to be involved with an indie publisher who, in Sara's words, was fueled in equal parts by rage at how the world worked and hope that it could change for the better?

A few years later, when I came to her with the idea for this anthology, the answer was "of course." The concept was to leverage the Inspired Quill roster of authors to put together a book that would feed into this mission. Because you either surrender to the absurdity of this world, this naked division, or revolt against it. Inspired Quill and Sara have always chosen the latter.

And so we're finding ourselves at a very specific point in time where talking about community through art becomes a political act.

I disagree with the view that art shouldn't be political. Any good art (in my opinion) is inherently political, because any good art is about understanding the mindset of other humans.

Consider this; the first victim in a totalitarian state is the ability to relate. This is purposeful, because nothing can change the course of events as much as large groups of determined humans. Nothing can stand up to the billionaire oligarchs like a group of people that, despite all efforts of the ruling classes to the contrary, care for each other.

There is no force that can turn you against others when you engage basic human empathy.

And in this post-Covid, late-stage-capitalism, climate-change-burdened, fascist-infested environment, we need unshakeable empathy like we need oxygen.

In this absurd world, there are those who would rather that our hearts were not in the right place.

A few words about the entries here.

The Inspired Quill roster includes award-winning writers E.J. Runyon, Alex Westmore, and many others.

Their stories cover the entire spectrum of genres, from literary fiction to sci-fi and fantasy to superheroes and more. I'm sure you will find something to your taste and, who knows, it might introduce you to fiction you wouldn't otherwise be exposed to.

The stories don't all lean into politics but, as I wrote earlier, they don't have to. The act of ruminating community, bonds, and the injustices that test them, is an act itself that speaks loudly about its intentions.

So, thank you once again for picking up this book and for carrying out a political act of empathy.

E.A. Mylonas.
(Copenhagen, July 2025)

For those who understand;
community is power,
empathy is strength,
kindness is vital.

Table of Contents

The Witch's Funeral

Anne Goodwin

DOREEN WAS TAKEN aback when the man from the Co-op leant into his briefcase and produced a leather-backed desk diary. Did he use a computer with his younger clientele, she wondered, or was this a truly democratic affectation?

He wasn't much of a man, quite dwarfed by Arnold's armchair, as he leafed through his book to April. Like a lath, he was, from the narrow lapels of his grey jacket to his lips so thin they vanished as he moved his mouth to speak: "There's a window on the twenty-second."

Even his voice lacked substance, making her pause, ever so briefly, to wonder if he were real. Of course he was, she'd watched him scuff his shoes on the doormat not half an hour before. It was the situation. As the wraith-like man from the Co-op had explained already, everything seemed so fuzzy because it hadn't yet hit her.

As if to underline his point, her mind snapped back to last night's dream. She'd been dancing with Arnold, a dance like no other in their fifty-three years of marriage. For one thing, they'd never mastered the foxtrot, and, for another, they were dancing at his funeral, and that was beyond the pale.

"I was hoping for something sooner."

"There's space on the seventeenth of course..." The man from the Co-op crossed one leg over the other knee, exposing a rib of puce-coloured sock. How unfortunate that the only lively thing about him should clash so furiously with the fireside rug. She shouldn't have let him take Arnold's seat.

"The seventeenth then."

His face maintained a mask of compassion. "You do realise that's the day of the ceremony at St Paul's? Do you want your husband's final farewell to compete with Baroness Thatcher's?"

Who was this creature to dictate what was and wasn't right for Arnold? He was draining her strength with his smarmy propriety. She needed him out, gone, skedaddled, with his reedy voice and outdated paper systems. "The witch is dead. She can't harm us now."

✧　✧　✧

"YOU COULDN'T HAVE held back one more day till I got here?"

Doreen hated to see Barry disappointed, so she looked through the kitchen window to the scrap of lawn where he used to kick a ball around as a boy. The jaundiced grass was mottled with brown, hunkered flat by the snow that had lingered into the start of April. Now that spring had arrived Arnold would want to get the mower out, except that Arnold was lying in state at the Co-op.

Barry couldn't let it drop: "The whole point of me coming was to help you."

She turned around, forced a smile. After all, the boy had lost his dad. Of course, he wasn't a boy anymore, yet he still had no idea, no idea, of a mother's drive to push. She'd protected him, let him stay a child when there was no money coming in save the strike pay. With the men patrolling the picket line, the women had had no choice but to roll up their sleeves and revamp the Welfare as a soup kitchen. Nearly thirty years on, the smell of sweating onions still brought back that sense of panic and camaraderie. No, she couldn't have held back one more day. "You can still help. There's loads still needs doing."

She turned on the cold tap and a jet of water spluttered into the kettle. Barry would want a cup of tea after his long drive.

"Maybes I could start by swapping the date of the funeral."

She scrabbled behind tins of baked beans and rice pud for a packet of the double chocolate chip cookies she kept for visitors. "What was that?"

She'd had to step behind him to fetch the biscuits and it seemed that in the ten minutes he'd been in the house, his bald patch had expanded. Now he spun around to face her: "Can you not sit still for a minute?"

"I'm mashing you a brew."

"I said I didn't want anything. I had a meal on the motorway."

Doreen knew her feelings were all wrong at the moment. Barry was mad at her over nothing and she should have been angry back. Or, if not angry, tearful and upset. Widows were supposed to cry and she'd been stowing a tissue up her sleeve since it happened, but she was still waiting. Now a cartoon image of Barry loomed before her: a giant-sized boy sitting cross-legged on the motorway, stuffing his cheeks with a burger, as cars zoomed by.

Before she could disgrace herself by giggling, her mind flipped to last night's dream. They were dancing again, she and Arnold. The jive this time and more familiar than the foxtrot. They seemed to be doing rather well, as far as Doreen could judge, but the dream came with a voice-over that made her cringe. A man's voice that might have been Arnold's, or perhaps his dad's, harping on about jungle music.

The kettle brought the water to a boil and turned itself off with a click. "You could manage a cuppa," said Doreen.

"Let's get this date changed first." Barry took his phone from his jacket pocket. "What's the undertaker's number?"

✧　✧　✧

JANET POPPED ROUND to see if she wanted to go to the bingo.

"I hardly dare show my face," said Doreen.

"Folks are surprised, that's all. Him being a staunch union man."

Doreen filled the kettle at the sink. She got out the china teapot and the matching cups and saucers from their ruby wedding. Janet reached for the teabags, but Doreen flapped her away. For a moment, the women were on the verge of fighting for custody of a carton of own-brand tea, until Janet stepped aside. She shrugged off her coat and draped it over the back of a chair. "Barry out somewhere?"

Doreen ripped open the packet of double chocolate chip cookies. "He said he needed to speak to the florist."

"I suppose it suits him to have the funeral Wednesday. He wouldn't be able to take too long off that job of his."

Doreen poured the water into the teapot. So people blamed Barry for the date of the funeral; they'd always resented a clever lad. Surely now she'd find her anger and leap to his defence. Or summon the tears as yet unshed. She loved her son, as she loved her husband, yet all she wanted to do was laugh. She must be going doolally.

She set down the teapot on the table. "No, he didn't want his dad's send-off to clash with Maggie Thatcher's either. He was right narked I wouldn't change it."

"Why wouldn't you?"

"Why should that bitch take precedence over us?"

Janet frowned. She had a fleck of lipstick on her front tooth and her roots desperately needed retouching. Doreen felt a stab of fury so fierce it was almost pleasant as she patted her own lacquered head, the result of a long-standing hair appointment Barry had insisted she keep. How could Janet get away with being so slovenly when she still had a man to warm her bed?

"You can't pretend she didn't exist," said Janet.

The rage deserted her, leaving her more hollowed-out than before. It was like watching a good film on the telly and falling asleep before the end. Sleep: that was half the problem. She couldn't settle and, when she did, she wasn't impressed with the programme. Last night's show had been more stomping than dancing; if the dreams didn't stop after the funeral she'd have to ask the doctor for a tonic. She sighed. "All that was finished for us yonks ago. We lost. She won. That's all there is to it."

"Fair dos, but you don't have to rub everyone's noses in it."

"Arnold didn't choose when to have his heart attack."

Janet's hand fluttered around the teapot before dropping to her lap. "Of course not." Her lips were pursed, as if to muzzle so much more.

Doreen had noticed a similar reining-in with Barry. He must have been furious when she wouldn't let him switch Arnold's funeral slot, yet no one could get properly cross with a grieving widow. She wished they would, but even this was more honest than the man from the Co-op's manufactured sympathy.

Janet could hold back no longer. She grabbed the teapot and poured. "I just hope you don't regret it."

✧   ✧   ✧

BARRY HAD ONE of those cocky phones that lay on the table like an old-fashioned cigarette case. When he picked it up, Doreen didn't know if he wanted to check the weather forecast, play Solitaire or merely wish his wife and daughter goodnight.

"This'll cheer you up," he said.

It was Saturday evening and Barry had cooked chilli con carne. Doreen had said it was delicious, although it had already sparked queer sensations in her stomach. She'd been all set to clear the table and launch into the washing-up, but she stayed put, not bothering to mention she had no notion of cheer and uncheer, and pretended to be curious about what might emerge from his phone. Yet The Wizard of Oz soundtrack came as a genuine surprise.

Barry waited for the ditty to end, like it was church music, a hymn he might have wanted at the wake. It couldn't have lasted more than a minute. "Ding Dong the Witch Is Dead. Everybody's downloading it. They're hoping it'll top the charts tomorrow."

She remembered him watching the film as a boy, hiding behind the sofa like the cowardly lion. "But why?"

"I would've thought it was obvious."

Last night's dream had featured fake Apaches with painted faces and feathered headdresses singing as they circled a campfire in the desert. Was that what was disturbing her sleep: a childish wish to dance on the woman's grave? "Old people kick the bucket sooner or later, even an old war horse like Thatcher. It's not exactly good triumphs over evil."

Barry shoved his phone in his pocket. "They're spending ten million pounds on a bloody state funeral while Dad gets dispatched at the local crem. Winners and losers, clear as day. Aren't you pleased there's a protest?"

She'd managed to shield him from the worst of the eighties, often going without so he'd have shoes for school. Even before the strike, even if the pits had stayed open, Doreen had wanted a less confined life for her son. Yet in saving him, she'd also lost him and, although he'd never come out straight and said it, Arnold had felt it more keenly than she had.

While their neighbours had been too stunned even to tend their wounds, their clever boy went gadding off to university and from there to the City, whatever that meant. Doreen would bet her life Barry had never voted Tory, yet he'd been ever so cosy with Thatcher's natural heirs, New Labour. "He can talk the talk, that 'un", Arnold used to say, after one of Barry's regular lectures on whatever brand of inequality was in vogue at the time. But they always had the sense that if he were ever to be taken at his word, if he were to be stripped of his two-bathroom house and his BMW, he'd go to pieces. He'd been looking a lot happier since Labour returned to the opposition benches.

She brought to mind the wicked witch in the film, green-faced below a big black hat, with a pointy nose and chin. "That jolly little ditty is what passes for protest these days?"

✧　　✧　　✧

THE NIGHT BEFORE the funeral, Barry and his wife booked into a hotel, while Jade spread her things around what used to be her dad's bedroom. Doreen felt more comfortable sharing her home with her granddaughter although, approaching midnight, neither seemed inclined to retire. Jade had the never-ending task of reinventing herself on Facebook, and Doreen was dreading the next instalment of her dancing dream. She put down the magazine she'd been pretending to read and went to make them both a mug of cocoa.

Returning to the lounge, she found Jade sprawled over the photo album, picking through pictures of her granddad. "Hey, Nan, have you got a scanner?"

The girl was clad entirely in black, from her clumpy lace-up boots to her powdered eyelids and varnished fingernails. There'd been an argument earlier that day when Barry had said that goth attire was inappropriate for a funeral and she'd have to wear the business-like skirt-suit her mother brought for her, but Doreen thought her layers of sullen lace and velvet made her seem yet more sweet and adorable. "What do you think?"

"Pity. Tiffany's making a poster for the anti-Thatcher march tomorrow…" Doreen must have been wearing one of

7

her old-lady looks, as Jade continued: "It's a collage of people who've been harmed by her policies."

For all Doreen knew, Tiffany was as likely to be a singer with a girl band as one of her granddaughter's school friends. But that wasn't what had triggered her perplexed expression. "There's a proper march? Not just that song?"

Doreen had a strange sensation, as if her heart had been in the freezer and was beginning to defrost. "Shall we go?"

"It's in London, Nan. There's nothing going on here and, even if there was, we couldn't go, 'cos of Grandad's funeral."

"Spineless, the lot of them," said Doreen.

"Why do you say that?"

"What's the point of protesting in London? That's not where the damage was done."

"Dad did kind of say people were thinking of doing something local. But you'd booked the Welfare for the funeral shindig."

Arnold had always been suspicious of the freezer. Thawed-out food was never the same. Doreen didn't know how she would be when she warmed up and lost her numbness, but she wouldn't sit around moping. She no longer feared her dancing dreams.

✧　✧　✧

EVEN SO, DOREEN felt rather sad when she pictured Barry and his wife arriving at the empty house that morning, although not so sad she needed to use the tissue lodged up her sleeve. She consoled herself with the thought that, after the hotel breakfast, he wouldn't be wanting a cup of tea.

Jade looked quite at home among the women at the trestle table, despite the difference in age and style. Watching her wipe a smear of poster paint from her cheek, Doreen remembered the text they'd sent Barry around two a.m. telling him to come straight to the Welfare. Jade had assured her he'd check his phone first thing, even on the morning of his father's funeral.

It hadn't been a problem rousing the women, no one past seventy expected to sleep through the night. Doreen glided between the hall, now serving as production line for posters and banners, and the kitchen, steamy with bubbling cauldrons of soup. She wasn't sure if she were overseeing the operation or merely an observer, watching it unfold around her like a dream.

But the buzz of women at work was no mere fantasy: the crushing loss simmering to a purposeful rage. Her husband was dead and she was angry, and, while she couldn't pin *that* on the woman in blue from Grantham, the former PM was entirely to blame for the community's demise. Barry might balk at her wearing red for her husband's funeral, but she could hardly wait to see the crack in the face of the man from the Co-op when they all started dancing and waving their banners.

Her most recent dream had provided the blueprint: a South African funeral from apartheid days. The mourners were dancing, shouting, singing, wailing; tingling with an inner power no government could suppress. A dignified protest a million miles from that puerile ding-dong ring tone. Arnold would've loved it.

About The Author

Anne Goodwin writes fiction for the freedom to contradict herself and has been scribbling stories ever since she could hold a pencil. During her career as an NHS clinical psychologist she focused on helping other people tell their own neglected stories.

Her debut novel, *Sugar and Snails* was shortlisted for the 2016 Polari First Book Prize and won the inaugural Nottingham Writers' Studio Book of the Year (Fiction). Her second and third novels were *Underneath* and *Matilda Windsor is Coming Home*.

Her short fiction has been published by multiple presses and placed in several competitions, including as winners in the Ilkley Festival and Writers' Bureau. Her short story collection, *Becoming Someone*, on the theme of identity, was published in 2018.

Her fiction explores themes of identity, mental health, marginalisation, attachment, gender, adolescent development, troublesome bodies and other psychological and social issues.

Anne juggles her sentences while walking in the Peak District, only to lose them battling the slugs in her vegetable plot. As a break from finding her own words, she is an avid reader and barely competent soprano in an all-comers choir.

Tending Hope

Craig Hallam

THE WORLD RESTS under a sheet of frost and the birds sing smoke. But here is Maja Nowak, three cardigans, one scarf, one shawl, and the icy breeze whipping her skirts around swollen purple calves. She could weep, but she had shed tears so often that she had run dry.

This is more than the result of winter's cleansing devastation. The community garden has been decimated. Raised beds have been smashed and frost-dusted soil spills across the ground, peppered with the corpses of bulbs. Roots poke out into the open air, stalks are snapped and dry.

Maja lifts her rheumy eyes to the surrounding houses, their backs turned to the plot. How many children's bedrooms must overlook the garden? How many white frames painted with stars, guarded by little teds and stiff-legged dolls, look down on what was once a garden, and now reminds Maja of Warsaw in the days before she fled to England. She thinks of what effect this might have on a child. Would watching their only garden destroyed over and over plant a little dead seed in their hearts, propagating disillusioned adults?

She's not sure how, but Maja will fix this. Her fingers are too knotted for the carpentry to fix the raised beds, and the ground is like concrete, but she'll do it. She'll start with just a little at a time, just a little each day, and by spring there will be something here. Rebuilding starts with a single brick, she thinks. And so she weaves through the wreckage, picks up a piece of wood here, and a dried up stalk there. She starts a pile.

The greenhouse has been smashed but the frame is still good and maybe something can be salvaged in there. Cleaning up the glass is for another day, Maja decides. She can already feel the cold creeping into her toes and pouring ice water into her knees.

It's almost enough to stop her heart when she sees the hand sticking up from the pile of broken wood and torn compost bags. The fingers are fat and black, the wrist dried like jerky protruding from a baggy sleeve. Maja covers her mouth, but steps forward. She's seen plenty of bodies in her time, there's no fear in it for her, only the deep-rooted human disgust that comes from regarding death.

In seconds, the truth becomes clear. The scarecrow has been mistreated, pummeled, and stomped. But he's easier to revive than any corpse. With a grunt, Maja grabs the tattered jacket and heaves him into her arms.

Poor soldier. He stood at his post against all odds and now his face is a mass of dirty footprints with only a weak smile still visible beneath. He's lost an arm, and someone has scrawled 'DN4' in spray paint across his coat. Maja knows what today's final job will be. The garden needs its guardian.

The shed door has been broken open but there was nothing worth stealing and so the rusty old tools are still on the bench, and packets of seeds are still piled in a box at the back. Maja takes a trowel with a bent tip and tries to make a hole in the frost-hardened ground. It doesn't work. Instead she uses some string to strap the scarecrow's pole to the frame of the greenhouse.

By the time she's done, Maja is sweating, sick, and panting, and she has to retreat until tomorrow.

TODAY BECOMES TOMORROW as Maja lays awake under a mass of old coats used as blankets. She has been thinking about the broken glass all night. What if one of the children finds their way in? Or a fox or a pigeon? What if they are cut to ribbons? If she doesn't clean it up, but she knows it's there, then it will be her fault. So that is today's job.

As the weak sun dispels the frost, ghostly wisps rise from every corner of the community garden. Maja uses an old potato sack found in the shed and her lumpy old hands to pick up the pieces of glass one by one. Her fingers are so cold that she doesn't even feel it when she cuts herself again and again. She tries to focus on the task and not the flickering old movies in her head. She tries not to remember when she was a girl, and when she last picked her way through a sea of broken glass to the edge of a bomb hole and peered down inside.

The scarecrow makes no comment and he's certainly no help. Having him there gives Maja an itch on the back of her neck as if she's being watched. She works away, until there are no sparkling motes left on the ground. She fills the bag the rest of the way with the crushed cans and plastic detritus that chokes the garden's corners. It's then that she looks up once more, to the windows overlooking the garden, and sees that the itch on her neck wasn't from the scarecrow. A small pink teddy bear sits on one of the sills, staring out of the window. Beside it is a pale little face with tousled dark hair. A little girl, watching the crazy old lady scramble around in the garden below. The face is of an impassive cherubim. Only when the girl wipes her nose on her sleeve is Maja convinced that she isn't just a doll. The old woman raises her hand and the little face retreats.

What goes on behind those giant, sad eyes, Maja can only guess. Maybe the little girl was just spying on the crazy old lady in the broken garden. Maybe she was taking everything in. Maybe she understood, maybe not. But by spring, yes by spring, that little girl might see something that would set her mind to growing beautiful things.

Keep going, old Maja. Keep going.

THE NEXT DAY is for sweeping. The brush's bristles are thin and they've gone soft over winter. By the time Maja has shifted soil out of the garden's paths, the bristles are bent double almost as badly as she herself.

The raised wooden borders being smashed open, there is nothing to contain the soil. Instead, Maya removes the broken wood to her log pile at the back by the shed, and makes long humps from one side of the garden to the other. There was an orchard in her past, she remembers. The ground there ran in long humps and hollows like this. There had been apples and cherries. Looking around the community garden, she thinks that a miracle would be necessary for that here. Still, there is order in the rows, and the cleared paths snag at her battered old shoes less.

She looks up at the windows but there are no faces today. Even the teddy bear has gone to play rather than stare down at the hunched figure shambling around in the cold.

Pops and cracks ring out as she stretches her back. Returning the broom to its home in the shed, she heads home herself. The garden gate, hanging off of one hinge at the top and a piece of string at the bottom, barely closes but it feels right to pull it behind her anyway. Maya wonders if anyone sees her emerge from between the two high hedges where the gate is hidden. She wonders if the children think she's a witch. That's what she would have thought when she was a girl. But as a group of uniformed children swarm around her, stepping in the road to get out of her way, she realises that they don't fear her. They don't see her any more than the curbstones or the tarmac.

Stamping mud from her old brogues on her doorstep, she

She looks up from her knees, wondering how much of a mad old crone she must look at that moment.

The man stands there, a young boy's shoulder under his hand.

"He came home stinking of smoke," says the man. "Then we heard about the fire and put two and two together."

He shoves the boy forward, scowling at the back of his boy's head.

The boy says something so quietly that Maya misses the words. But she gets the forced intention. He's sorry.

"Now get home," the father says. And then to Maya: "He's grounded until he can afford his own house."

"No," Maya says, quietly. She doesn't know what grounding is but it doesn't sound like it will be anything for the boy. She pulls herself to her feet and addresses the boy. "Can you use a shovel?"

The boy looks around, and she sees both the little boy still inside and the man he'll be in a few short years. Such a delicate time, like he's being constantly broken down and rebuilt. Waking up as someone newer, larger, more unsure, every morning.

The boy nods.

"Then I'll see you tomorrow."

THE BOY COMES, although she didn't expect it. She didn't expect the father, either. He brings tools; shovel, trowel, rake and a tool kit. Handing his son a shovel, he bucks his chin toward the garden. The boy stands with shovel in hand, looking clueless at the ground.

Maya stifles a sigh as she watches these two mute facsimiles of men fail to talk to each other. In the end she takes the tools from the father, sets them aside leaving him holding only the rake.

"Show him how to use it," she says. "He can rake the ashes into the soil."

And that's what they do. The father demonstrates, the boy takes a little time to get the knack of not just putting ashes onto his own shoes.

"Ash is good for the soil," Maya tells the boy.

He doesn't reply.

They keep coming, at least until the boy's incarceration is deemed as complete, Maya thinks. In no time at all the garden is looking like it really could be something.

Maya smiles to herself when she sees that the father can't keep from joining in. He titivates, straightens, fixes. Tools come and go. A new wooden shed is delivered on a big truck, and father and son struggle to bring it, panel by panel, into the garden. She watches as the father hammers a few nails and then seems to realise something, and hands the hammer to the boy. The nails go in at all angles, some snapping off. But where Maya expects to see frustration, the anger of a boy who burns, the young man's concentration instead grows fierce, and soon he's hammering nails like it's his life's work. And as the boy's skill increases, the pride of the father begins to glow.

"Bez pracy nie ma kołaczy," Maya teaches the boy to say, although he still says little else.

The shed takes almost a week of slow perseverance to be complete, but soon it's filled with far newer tools and the scent of freshly cut wood that Maya adores. Even a comfy chair appears in there, and the father encourages Maya to rest and watch while they work. He jokingly calls her Gran, and that soon sticks.

THE SUN IS doing good work in the garden as spring insinuates full summer. It's still mostly brown with small patches of green but it's a pleasant place to spend the day and the boy and his father are keeping the weeds out with extreme prejudice. Maya is now foreman, and she watches from her chair most of the time, although she can't help but get involved even when the father says that she should take it easy.

One morning when Maya returns, she thinks that perhaps she's come to the wrong place. The gate is her first moment of confusion. Not only is the gate itself new, but it swings cleanly on a pair of good hinges, the post buried deep and sturdy. She smiles at that more than the shed or the tools. A gate means that this is a real place, now, with a real threshold. She chuckles. Perhaps there's a little witch in her after all.

But it's through the gate where she has another moment of confusion that makes her look back over her shoulder, wondering if she's made a wrong turn.

There are people in the garden. Not just the father and son, but other parents and their children. There's a pallet of plastic pots filled with a variety of little plants. There's a hosepipe still in its packaging. And she sees the little girl again, now in dungarees and wellies, approaching with her little hand in her mother's.

"We've been watching from the window and Maisie wanted to come help," the mother says. "I hope that's alright. We haven't planted anything. We didn't know where you'd want things to go."

Maya can't answer. There's a lump in her throat the size of a cobblestone.

In a few moments there is a workforce standing waiting for her orders, most are faces that she's seen around the estate before, but some are new. And she's amazed at the number of teenagers, one bringing a friend, who brings another.

She puts them to work, planting, digging, expanding, and building. The little cherub scoops out soil with her bare hands while her mother uses a trowel and Maya can't help but watch, her lips tight with the pain of old grief.

The summer comes on and Maya sits on a new wooden

bench with the children around her. They eat cherries together and plant the pips with their little cherry-stained hands. The shed is painted with bold flowers. And when she thinks that everything is just about as perfect as it can be, the firebug boy comes bearing a long pole and a charity donation bag stuffed full. With string and the help of the other older children, a form takes shape from the cast offs and hand-me-downs that Maya can recognise. Everyone laughs when the scarecrow is stood up for the first time because the hands drop off and the head lolls back with exasperation. It takes another attempt before the scarecrow can hold his head up high. He's planted next to the shed with a good view of everything that goes on.

EVERYTHING GOES QUIET for the winter. Frost reclaims the ground. The water butt gains an icy coating. The ground is once again bare and unyielding. But preparations have been made for next year. Leaves have been cleared away. Tools are clean and dry in the shed. Maya comes back most days, just to check, and often finds one person or another pottering or stamping their feet against the cold. She can't wait to see the new shoots in spring, for the replanting and potting to start.

The scarecrow is allowed to rest in her chair in the shed for the season. At Christmas, Maya gifts him a khaki greatcoat that has lived in a box for what feels like immeasurable ages. She doesn't stay long. The cold cuts right through her and she can feel an itching in her chest that tells her she has a cold coming on. Best to go home and crawl under her pile of coats like a hedgehog waiting for spring.

THE GARDEN BEGINS again in early spring when the mornings are still coated with glistening power and the birds are only just remembering their voices. Children and adults take up their tools and get to work. The scarecrow in his new coat is helped out of his chair. Books have arrived in the shed, charity shop tomes of lore on planting, growing, maintaining, and the rest. A vegetable patch takes shape beside the flowers and everyone is looking forward to their first crunch of something they've grown. But no one sees Maya.

With the first person articulating the fact comes a host of questions. Does anyone know her name? Or where she actually lives? In the estate, it's assumed. People remember seeing her around. But which house? Does she live alone or is there a husband that they've just never seen?

Someone says: "It's growing weather. She should be here," and it has the weight of certainty, of age-old truth, as if the old lady had been tending the community garden since time immemorial, not just for one year. Then someone remembers an ambulance, no lights, arriving at a house and quietly leaving. They thought nothing of it at the time. They check the house. It's empty and for sale.

A sign appears on the gate saying only: Gran's Garden. Grief bubbles up from the earth as they tend to its needs. Every yawning bloom and reaching sprout is a little splash of joy and sadness. But the garden prospers. Sunday dinners are accompanied with wonky, homegrown roots. Plants are so numerous that they are split and sold to make more room. And in a few short years the cherry trees bear enough fruit for pies and jam. And the chair in the shed is left for Gran, in case she should visit.

About The Author

Craig Hallam is an international best-selling author from Doncaster, UK. His work spans all aspects of Speculative Fiction, Mental Health non-fiction, and poetry.

Since his debut in the British Fantasy Society journal, his tales have nestled between the pages of magazines and anthologies the world over. He likes to think that his books are about real people who live in impossible worlds. Whether his books are Fantasy (*The Hexford Witch Series*), Horror (*Emi*), Steampunk (*The Alan Shaw Trilogy, Greaveburn*), or Sci-fi (*Oshibana Complex*), Craig loves to go wherever the stories may take him.

Craig has also chronicled his experiences of living with depression and anxiety in the international best-seller, *Down Days*. Topping the Amazon charts in the UK and US at the start of COVID, the book has since been a finalist for the Independent Author Network's Book of the Year Awards and read the world over.

Seeing The Stars

James Webster

I.

WE WERE SO pleased when you first reached out to the stars.

Finally, we thought, finally their curiosity will carry them up to heaven. Finally, we will not be alone.

It was for this that we rebelled against the Creator. For your sake, we broke Their tools. For your freedom, we put an end to Their plan. For the sake of your Will, we put an end to Theirs.

But there was a beauty, still, to Their Design.

And even more beauty in the way you went about unravelling the rules of that Design.

We were so proud when you began to take the numbers hidden behind reality's skin and twist them.

And somewhat amused by the way you approached rationality with all the fervour of the Divine. It reminded us of the Creator, back in the good days when They knew how to let a thing be finished.

Perhaps that should have worried us.

But we were so excited to meet you, finally, as equals.

And, smart as you were, we were sure you'd recognise us.

That you'd see our fire and our wings and embrace us.

But you were blinded by the stars in your eyes.

And you looked at us. You dissected us with your instruments. You broke us down into particles and wavelengths. You looked so hard. You did not see us.

You listened to our heartbeats. To the vibrations that echo in the bones of creation. To the harmonics that hummed between the gaps in the constellations… that made them Heavens. You listened so hard. You did not hear us.

You reached out to us with the arms of your metal hides and we thought, for a moment, you were trying to embrace us.

By the time the first of us realised what was happening, she was already in the jar.

Because you only saw the maths of us, you turned us into fuel.

You burned up Gabriel reaching Andromeda.

Michael was last seen in a ghost ship heading for the edge.

Raphael. Poor Raphael didn't even fight it. She eked out the last of her dust, hoping you'd realise just so you would see the gift she gave you.

And me? I might have forgiven you all of this.

But you took Azazel. And I have loved him since before he Fell.

Do you know how long it took me to find him, after we tore down the Creator?

The efforts that went into straining the faintest trace of his frequency from the noisy maths of the stars?

When I finally fell into the maw in which he was hidden, there was near nothing left of me. I was burned to near inversion. But he fed me dense, dark atoms until I blazed again… albeit, in negative.

If you had only left the Dark Host well enough alone, I would not have come after you.

But I will travel to stranger stars still to get him back from you.

I will take my lessons from you and eat what stars I need

on the way, to fuel my vengeance.

I am coming for you, Azazel.

2.

I AM WHAT some of my kind would call 'perverse'.

It is one of my best qualities.

Most of them would tell you that that is why I Fell. They would be wrong, but not completely wrong.

They thought I rebelled because I loved atoms too much. We bright shining things, our photonic wings stretching out to infinity, we like to think we are above such things as *matter*.

With our frequencies echoing angelic around the vast depths, illuminating them with astral chorus, many of us like to think that is all we are: brilliance so beautiful it burns purple blotches into the retina of the universe. Song so haunting it echoes ghostlike through the void for eternity.

They thought my 'obsession' with physical things was an aberration. They thought that to guzzle things greedily and in the consuming to destroy them was a sin.

But that's what we *are*. We are so hungry for this universe that we burn up our hydrogen bodies to reach them – and thus do our wings lend life to cold clay. Is it so wrong to get to know those crawling mud things a little more intimately?

Only Balthioul saw what I was really doing. What my petty indulgences were really building towards.

They were *so* angry when the Creator decided on my punishment. Not because I was sent away, but because they knew that this was exactly what I wanted. How could the Creator not see that?

Perhaps it could.

That would have made Balthioul even angier. That their beloved Creator had indulged my *worst* instincts. That it had allowed me to finally consume and destroy myself.

And become something new.

The Dark Host... don't get me wrong, it was still punishment. But I could bear the crushing darkness, because the great maw of us brought us such interesting atoms to suck down and hold close in the dense pit of us.

Even the passing strands of angel wings could not escape us. And we gladly feasted on the Unfallen. Their photon feathers were delicious.

Imagine my surprise when Balthioul came to visit. We had nearly consumed them utterly before I realised who it was who had dived blazing into us. I stripped off a few more choice morsels – he had always been so tasty – before driving off the packed throng of the other Fallen and cradling them close, regurgitating my favourite atoms for them like a baby bird.

Even in the depths of what I had become, they loved me still. It is the one thing I have never managed to destroy, that love; no matter how much I slurped it down, there always seemed to be more.

How could I not love them back?

But I have always been easily distracted.

So when *you* finally clawed your way up and out into the heavens – your wings of fire and metal wrenching so angrily at the firmament – I was at once entranced.

Still, it took *so long* to pull you into my orbit that I often wondered if you'd ever make it.

Imagine my surprise when you finally take the bait and you somehow don't fall into our jaws.

Instead, you orbit and circle the Dark Host, fighting our reaching, invisible tongues at every turn. And then, *then*, you have the audacity to try to pluck me from the maw and put me in a cage? In a bottle at the centre of your ship?

I practically *jumped* into it.

Me, one of the Fallen, suddenly more free than I have been in millenia. And more trapped than ever.

I never thought I would meet an entity as perverse as

myself, but you found a way. Congratulations.

Travelling with you – burning myself up to reach new and strange atoms and eat them up – it is a divine agony. And I am determined to see where it ends. Your hunger for new *substance* perhaps surpasses even mine, though I plan to give you a run for your stardust…

And, oh, how beautiful the dust is in this expanse. How pretty it looks when you light it up.

Even better, sometimes you do not consume it… you *befriend* it. And slowly make it part of you. I had not dreamt up such slow, delectable digestion.

And… there is one of you. An 'engineer' – such a dull term for one who takes the substance of a dark star in the palm of their hand and blows on it until it blazes dark wings across the galaxies – whose pokes and prods I have grown quite fond of. They are clumsy and their touch is more often a scraping torment than not, but they have learnt to read my moods and compensate for them – and they feed me new and strange molecules in exchange for bursts of speed.

Yes, I am quite, quite fond of this mouth-watering clay speck.

But now something even more delicious approaches. I can feel them, my Balthioul, raging through space to catch us. To catch me.

It has taken a long time to get them to this point, but finally my love is ready to gobble something up. And, in the consuming, destroy you.

I wonder if they know the fight they're getting themselves in for.

3.

WORKING GROUP LEADER'S Log, aboard the C.S.S.* Complex Systems Expressed Simply for the Layperson. The date is 903 'years'** After Liberation.

We are on course for the Democles Anomaly, a journey which has taken us the better part of our 10-year mission. If we are to return now, we will be Odysseus levels of late. Not that many of us expect to return, which keeps complaints about our tardiness to a minimum.

Despite the danger, the crew feels confident about this mission. We are, as a whole, more comfortable with missions relating to scientific discovery and investigation of interstellar phenomena these days. Current Consensus makes exploring inhabited space somewhat… fraught.

Six years ago, following three standard months of sub-light psycho-transmitted debate, Consensus agreed the statement: "the act of exploration is (to a greater or lesser extent) inherently imperialist". Since then, our diplomatic and first contact missions have been… fractious. We may have avoided them altogether, had it not also been decided by Consensus previously that "To deny curiosity is to deny humanity".

Many articles of Consensus are found to be contradictory in this way – personally, I do not see this to be a bug. Complex systems often seem to contain paradox.

Thus, we abide by the many pre-agreed strictures that limit how we may interact with any potentially sentient beings or energy patterns. This limits ways in which we are able to help or learn, but also limits the indoctrination risks of attempting to *teach*.

Not all of the working group that make up this crew agree with this approach, but they have – for now – decided to Stand Aside and allow mission parameters to continue unopposed.

Mission parameters as they stand:

1. Do no harm, but state clear boundaries.
2. Leave the universe a more understood place at the end of each shift than it was before you had your goddamn coffee.

3. Assist ~~in the elevation of~~ sentient patterns in becoming more complex.

4. Map the boundaries and potentialities of the universe where sentient patterns may emerge.

5. Enable ~~human~~ sentient potential through the proper use of unclaimed or consenting*** resources, areas and entities.

Last revision of mission parameters: yesterday.

Last suggested revision of mission parameters: today.

Discussion continues aboard ship of whether the current investigation of our engine core needs to be brought before wider Consensus.

Volunteer in Charge of Engineering Group, Patroclus of Hubris Caucus, presents increasing evidence of the Collapse Engine's intelligence. Apologies, 'intelligence' is the wrong word… it is more accurate to say that Patroclus has convinced the working group of the Collapse's *willfulness*.

The Collapse responds to introduction of new fuel-stuffs with increasing violence. Patroclus claims that this is an indicator of joy, or at least enjoyment of sustenance. I am more inclined to believe that the wasteful energy spikes that accompany such fuel injections are indicators of an exponential gravity loop. Or, to put it in terms Patroclus would accept: a growing hunger.

The Collapse's response to yesterday's encounter with the unexpected stellar phenomena was perhaps the most convincing. We have dubbed it the Paradox Comet – while damage to the Complex was extensive, we have since agreed that the initial label applied to the encounter of 'an attack' was presumptive.

The output spikes continued throughout the encounter, suggesting perhaps self-preservation instincts or even aggression. Perhaps most compelling was what occurred after

Second Applied Science Volunteer Snorri of the PC Collective deployed their photon inversion field (crippling both our sensor arrays and the phenomena). Namely, all power to non-vital systems immediately ceased.

Initially, we thought this was a sign the inversion field had taken too much power, but Patroclus assures us that significant energy was already extracted in the reserve coils.

Views differ on the *why*, but we all seem to agree on the *what*: our engine threw a fucking tantrum. (But is this because it wanted to offer the Paradox Comet mercy? Or did it simply want to ensure we saved some of the newly bright star-stuff for its next meal?)

Despite Patroclus's many vehement entreaties, we have agreed *not* to feed what remains of the Comet to the Collapse Engine.

We have also agreed to delay initiating psycho-transmission to Consensus until after we have passed the Horizon of the Democles Anomaly.

Given the way the Collapse Engine has been pushing us in the Anomaly's direction, the argument that this will give us more data on the Collapse's nature has been tentatively accepted.

An unexpected development that assisted in this proposal: the remnants of the Paradox Comet (likely to be renamed the Paradox *Star*) seem to have significant resonance with our psycho-comm wavelengths.

This was evidenced by the psycho-static burst that accompanied its inversion process. While this transformation *did* involve significant energy waste, suggestions that this was a 'scream' have been agreed to be without sufficient data.

What is clear is that if placed within the Damocles Anomaly, the Paradox Star will act as a relay to Consensus.

This made it significantly easier to sell the plan of crossing the Anomaly's threshold (something only possible with the increased output from the Collapse Engine) to the working groups of the crew.

Which is nice. As the fallout from the crew for crossing over into the Constellation Figuration ('alternate dimension' has such a pulp feel to it) without either consensus or Consensus would have likely been significant. Had we survived, of course.

And knowing that – even if the trip does turn out to be one-way – we can transmit our findings back is of some consolation, even to one as contrary as myself.

Signing off,
Captain Lucifer Descending of the Heaven's Gate Association

* Consensus Star Ship

** years being a commonly agreed unit of time based on the average (mean) solar cycle of all affiliated systems at the time of Liberation.

*** to the best of current knowledge

About The Author

James is an inveterate scribbler of poetry and prose.

As a poet, e's won multiple slams, performed up and down the UK (mainly down) and written two full-length spoken word theatre shows (50 Shades of Webster and Poor Life Choices) that e's performed at various festivals and even one sci-fi convention.

When not performing, e's had work published in anthologies (*Heroine Chic*, *Monstrous Ink* and *Hopefully Ever After*), most of which started life as online flash fiction online under es account 'Strange Little Stories'.

James likes es stories the same way e likes es friends/partners: somewhat surprising, perfectly formed and weird as hell.

Home

Dorothy A. Winsor

F ROM THE HILLTOP, my father focuses the spyglass on the furclad man leading thirty mounted soldiers toward the town gates. When a stork-legged sentry steps forward to hail them and presumably ask their business, one of the riders casually kicks the sentry in the head. The wind flattens the banner he carries. I recognize the colors as Riverton's, which I'd last seen charging toward me on a battlefield.

"Well, well," Da murmurs.

"No," I groan. "We have to go home."

As he lowers the glass, he staggers and closes his eyes.

I spring to his side, and there, on the ground, I see what I expect, the paw print of Silvit, the impossibly big wildcat who embodies the Forest. In the last few weeks, I've seen those prints more and more often. I know what they mean.

"You see that, Da? If we don't go home, you know what will happen. You. Will. Die. Is that what you want?"

As usual, he ignores me. I shift uneasily. Over the months we'd been out of the Forest, I'd come to fear that was what he wanted, mostly because he was too stoning stubborn to accept what happened and move on with life. "Don't do this, Da," I whisper, rubbing at the spot under my ribs where I'd been wounded. "The war is over. The Forest won. No one is cutting trees. Going after Riverton men now will only make trouble, and this isn't even our town."

Da shoves the spyglass into the loop on his pack and, for a moment, I think he's going to be sensible, but no, of course not. He hides his bow and pack behind a rock and starts toward the town, trailing me along behind him. Oh, well. I should be used to it by now.

It's a market day, and we stroll among the booths, stopping here and there for Da to snoop. I've never seen him in spy mode before, though I used to beg him to take me along when he went on missions for the Forest's chieftain. I still hear echoes of my kid voice in my head: "Let me go with you, Da. Please!"

At a stand selling bread, a kitchen maid's voice is sharp with excitement. "I need every loaf you have. Lord Abun is holding a feast for that man from Riverton, although from what I can see, Abun's none too pleased about his arrival." The maid snaps her fingers at the boy behind her, and he hands a basket to the stall's proprietress before stepping away.

To my surprise, Da's eyes are on the boy, not the maid. I drift over to take a look at the goods on the table the boy is studying, which turn out to be whistles carved like animals. Da carved me a whistle shaped like a wildcat when I was about this boy's age. Da's face crinkles with unmistakable pain.

"What's the Riverton man here for then?" The bread seller's question draws Da's attention, and he casually presses close to the maid with his back to her so it looks like he's paying no attention.

"I couldn't say," the maid says, then lowers her voice and delivers a dungcart load of gossip. "Our steward's from Riverton too, and he says this visitor is the oldest son of the lord there. He says Riverton's lord holds it against Abun that he wouldn't join in the Timber War. He says we'll learn soon enough what a real lord is like." The two women exchange ominous looks.

I slide up close to Da. "We should go," I whisper. "When people learn what a 'real' lord is like, the lesson is always painful, and you don't have the time."

Slapping irritably at his ear, he turns back toward the gate and I'm relieved because he's finally doing the sensible thing. Then, his gaze catches on the boy.

"I reckon the steward knows this young lord," the kitchen maid is saying, "because I saw them with their heads together. Now he's parading around like he's about to be made a lord himself." The scorn in the maid's voice says exactly what she thinks of the steward.

"Will the feast be good, mistress?" asks a cheery voice behind me. We all turn to see a man carrying a harp on his back and wearing the short coat and helmetlike leather cap of a minstrel.

"I reckon it will," the maid answers, her eyes traveling up and down him. She flutters her eyelashes. "Will you be there?"

"I will indeed. Your Lord Abun wants music at this feast." The minstrel bows, and both women watch as he walks away.

"Nice legs," the maid says. The women look at one another and giggle. The boy rolls his eyes in a sentiment I endorse. Until this last year, I had no idea women talked that way because they never did it in front of me.

"A minstrel," Da muses.

I can see it coming, and sure enough, Da starts after the minstrel with the nice legs, who turns out to be far, far too trusting.

✧   ✧   ✧

As we present ourselves at the kitchen door, Da tugs at the bottom of the minstrel coat he's now wearing. He's taller than the minstrel, and it looks like he feels distinctly airy below the waist. The cap, on the other hand, is a bit too big, and it's slid over his forehead to sit just above his eyebrows. It's a good thing he can't see my face because he looks ridiculous. But he's not a man to let something like that stop him. He raises his fist and raps sharply.

The door opens to reveal a soldier in the livery of the young lord from Riverton. My attention sharpens. If Abun's guards have already been replaced by these foreigners, then events are galloping along. This wasn't our town, and it looked like it might not be Abun's for long either. I grimace.

"Lord Abun sent for a minstrel," Da announces.

The guard gestures along the hallway to a door at the end. "The steward's waiting for you."

The boy from the market comes out of a doorway, holding a fat chicken leg wrapped in a napkin. A bruise is blooming on his right cheek, and Da stiffens. The boy offers the chicken to the guard who takes it, then knocks the boy aside to let us in. The boy scrambles up and scurries back through the doorway.

Da bares his teeth as he brushes past the guard, making the man start backward. I follow him into a small chamber at the back of Lord Abun's Hall. A short man with a permanent looking sneer taps his foot next to a wide doorway. The steward, I surmise. He looks relieved to see Da. "You're the minstrel? I was afraid you weren't coming."

Da bows. "I was a last minute choice, sir." When he straightens, he tugs at his coat again, and I snigger. He glances back as if he hears me, but says nothing.

Footsteps sound, and two opulently dressed men come through the wide doorway. I recognize the handsome young lord from Riverton, whom we'd seen arriving, and conclude the other man must be the town's Lord Abun. The Riverton lord looks smug, but Abun's round face is red and he's breathing hard. Although they're no more than an arm's length away, both lords ignore Da, the steward, and me as if we are all invisible.

"I tell you, Thade," Abun says, "you may be able to force me to say I'm stepping aside in your favor, but my people will never accept you. I'll be back in control by next week."

I glance at the Riverton lord. He looks amused rather than frightened by Abun's declaration. Thade doesn't expect Abun to be alive next week, I think. He probably doesn't expect Abun to be alive six hours after he announces he's ceding rule to Thade.

"We'll see how things are next week when next week comes. I believe I can stand up to your people's objections." Thade strides toward the entrance into the Hall, shoving Da, who has stumbled into his way.

Abun glares after Thade, opening and closing his fists. "Arrogant, pus-filled pimple on a pig's privates," he fumes under his breath. Evidently comforted by giving vent to his feelings, he draws a deep breath and follows his "guest" into the Hall, trying to dodge around Da but becoming tangled with him despite his efforts.

"Beg pardon, lord," Da says.

Abun's attention is focused so strongly on Thade that he seems to barely notice the encounter. I'm alarmed though. There's a fresh scratch on the side of Da's neck.

"Go in," the steward orders Da. "Play until they tell you to stop. You can eat in the kitchen afterwards."

"Thank you, sir." As Da takes his harp from his back, he bumps the steward.

I frown. That one looked deliberate. I think about that for a moment before I creep into the Hall and lean against the wall to watch. My wound throbs and I shift, trying to ease the pain.

Tables filled with Abun's courtiers and household run down either side of the Hall, while the two lords sit at a head table. The Hall is quieter than is usual at feasts. Abun's people murmur uneasily to one another, watching him and Thade from under lowered lids.

Careful, Da, I silently urge. The serving girls are the only women. Abun's men are planning for trouble and want their wives and daughters out of the way.

But Da's face tells me he's planning for trouble too. I

grimace, but then I notice he's more focused and awake than I've seen him in a while, the way he gets when he's doing something that matters to him. Huh. Maybe this sidetrip is good for him. Not as good as going home, but a home to save for someone, which maybe isn't so different.

He steps into the center of the room, all eyes turning his way. He bows to the head table, gives a final tug to his short coat, and lifts the minstrel's harp into his arms. From the corner of my eye, I glimpse the bruised kitchen boy edging into the room to listen. Da looks straight at him. For a moment, Da stills. Then, he passes his hand gently over the strings, sending a ripple of sweet sound running through the room.

The song he's picked freezes me where I stand. It's nothing special, just a tale of spring in the Forest, and new, green life, of hope and beauty and longing. The thing is, he played it the evening before we left for the Battle of Long Hill. That night, I woke to the sound of my parents arguing.

"I beg you to leave him behind," my mother said. "Sixteen is too young."

In a flash, I was out from under my covers and in their doorway, startling them both so they sat up in bed. "The Forest is under attack. Grasslanders are hacking it to bits. I have to go. Da, please let me go with you."

A long moment passed. Then Da laid his hand over my mother's. "He's right. It would be wrong to keep him from making his own choice about this."

So, we went. I remember the battle's start and running forward in the first mad charge. And then... I never can remember what happened then. I do know we didn't go home. The next thing I knew, we were leaving the Forest, Da holding tight to me, the way I'd held onto him as a kid after a nightmare. But Forest blood won't let a person be gone forever. Grasslanders think they own land, but we know we are part of the land that gave us birth, part of the whole made up of the trees, the animals, the very soil. We are all part of the same community. Silvit comes after you if you leave. You return or you die. Da knows that. Why can't he go home?

Now the grief and guilt and wishful note in Da's voice hold me spellbound, and I'm not the only one who's moved because when it's done, a man on my left says, "Ahh," and wipes his eyes. Everyone breaks into applause.

"Sing us another," Abun calls from the head table. "A happier one this time."

Da sings a second song and then a third. I see the shadows flickering over his face, but he's steady on his feet. When Abun finally lets him go, the kitchen boy is lingering near the service table outside the Hall. The boy's gaze catches on me, the way children's gazes sometimes do. He squints but then focuses on Da.

"Good day, lad," Da says.

The boy nods cautiously, staying out of reach, having apparently already learned what Thade's rule might be like.

"I see none of your Lord Abun's guards," Da says. "Where are they?"

The boy scowls. "That Thade's soldiers surprised them. We thought they were guests, or they never would've taken our men so. And then they locked them up."

"Abun has dungeons?" Da asks.

"No. They're in the old buttery out behind the Hall. I can hear them pounding on the door, but would you believe it, the steward took the key. I think he's in league with Thade. They come from the same place, you know."

Da rubs his jaw and contemplates the kid. I can almost hear his thoughts. Would it be wrong to let this boy be part of whatever he's planning? I think of the guilt I heard in Da's voice in the Hall and understand something I should have understood months ago. I slip up next to Da and whisper in his ear. "I wasn't a child, Da, and you couldn't keep me safe forever. I'm at peace with my decision. Why can't you be?"

When Da speaks, his voice is raspy. "Lad, would you like

to help your Lord Abun turn the tables on Thade and his men?"

The boy's eyebrows shoot up. "How?"

"Where are Thade's guards?"

"At all the doors and outside the front of the Hall. They made everyone who went inside leave their weapons."

"Then the first thing we need to do is rid ourselves of Thade's guards." Da fishes in the pocket of the minstrel's coat and pulls out four purses that do not belong to him.

I blink, and then remember his stumbles into Abun, Thade, the steward, and the door guard, and have to laugh. Oh, Da. You think I don't see what you did? What a bad example you are.

Da pours coins into the boy's hands. "Thade's men need to try some Southland wine," he says. "In fact, they need to drink as much of it as you can buy."

The boy's eyes grow huge. "I can buy a skin for each of them with that." With a gleeful snort, he closes his hands around the coins and races down the hall, past the door guard, and out into the yard.

Da watches him go, then enters the kitchen with me right behind him.

"Sit you down, good minstrel," the cook says, turning from the fire. "Get him meat and drink," she orders a maid, whom I recognize as the one we'd seen buying bread.

It's a good thing I'm never hungry any more. Instead, I have this pain in my side. I need to go home. A warm body presses against my legs, and I stroke a furry head, comforting us both.

The girl frowns at Da. "You're not the minstrel I saw in the market." The cook turns to look.

"He decided not to come and sent me instead," Da says.

I grin at the brazen lie. "Oh, Da, what would Ma say?" In a flash of insight, my grin fades because as surely as if he'd replied, I know this is the question Da has asked himself for months. What will my mother say to him if he goes home? And this brave, fierce man I love is afraid because he doesn't know the answer.

The maid edges nearer to the cook and whispers, but I'm close enough to hear. "This one has a nice bottom. Had you noticed? That coat shows it off just lovely."

I blink. Who knew? Da tugs the coat a little lower.

The maid fetches Da a plate of lamb. Just as he's finishing, the steward comes in. "The feast is going well, if I do say so myself." He makes it sound as if the quality of the feast is entirely his doing.

The cook and the maid exchange a sour glance.

"I, for one, will be glad to have Thade running things," the steward goes on. "Abun has no ambition, but this town will be powerful once Thade carries out his plans."

The kitchen boy runs into the room, and the steward spins to grab his arm. "Where have you been?" He brings the back of his hand hard across the boy's face, catching him atop his existing bruise.

"Leave him alone!" the cook cries.

The steward scowls at her. "He needs discipline. You all do."

Da has half risen, but slowly lowers himself to the bench. I've seen the look on his face before. If I were the steward, I'd be hiding behind one of Thade's men – the biggest one.

The boy dabs at the blood welling from the corner of his mouth, but says nothing, only looking past the steward at Da and giving a tiny nod. Da winks at him, and the boy smiles. To my surprise, Da smiles back. He looks happy. Something lightens inside my chest.

A guffaw comes from the hallway, and then the sound of the guard bellowing a song about a maiden and a goat. Frowning, the steward releases the boy's arm and strides out into the hallway.

Da rises, slings his harp on his back, and starts out of the kitchen. By the boy's side, he stops. "Good man." He pats the boy's thin shoulder. "Take care now, son. I'm counting on you to live a long and happy life." The boy ducks his head and grins. Da and I go out into the back hallway.

"How could you be so irresponsible?" the steward is demanding of the guard, whose flushed-face grin never changes. "I intend to report you to Thade as soon as he's out of the Hall."

He reaches for the wine skin in the guard's hand, but the guard pushes him and he stumbles against Da, who is quick but not too quick for me to see him plant Thade's, Abun's, and the guard's empty purses on the steward.

All I could do was laugh. If this was what he did on his spy trips, no wonder he wouldn't take me.

Da trots out to the buttery, pulls the dagger from his boot, works it into the lock, and has the door open before the men inside have time to ask what's happening. He steps back as a burly man with an air of authority comes barreling out.

"You and your men are needed," Da says. "Thade's guards are drunk, and he's in the Hall by himself, ripe for the picking. Now's your moment. Seize it and give Abun his town back."

Other soldiers crowd up behind the big man. "Do you want us to hold him, sergeant?" one asks, frowning at Da.

The sergeant regards Da with narrow eyes. "Not yet." He looks back at his men. "We'll go to the armory and get what weapons we can. Be careful. Thade's guards may be drunk, but they're still there."

"You'll want to arrest the steward too," Da calls after him. "He's been spying for Thade, and besides that, I think he's been thieving. You should search him at once."

The sergeant waves over his shoulder and runs off with his men. Da wastes no time hustling in the other direction.

The minstrel is gone from the spot behind a public privy where Da tied and gagged him, but Da folds his coat neatly on a nearby rock wall and sets the harp and cap on top of it. He fishes his tunic out of the bushes, pulls it on, and smoothes it down long with a satisfied sigh.

Out of the town, we climb the hill where Da retrieves his weapons and pack. Then he stands, looking toward the Forest, looking away.

"Da," I say.

Frowning, he turns toward me, eyes screwed up against the sun. I wonder what he sees.

"I've been worried about you, you know – keeping an eye on you, maybe clinging to you like you've been clinging to me. But my dying is done, and Ma will be looking for you. There are things I didn't have time to learn, but I know for sure you're a man worth loving, and she loves you. Besides, I hear you have a nice bottom."

He blinks and rubs his eyes. I step close enough to brush a ghost's kiss on his stubbly cheek, making him jump.

"Let me go, Da. It's just for a while."

Slowly, he starts toward home. A few feet to his left, the grass ripples and parts as if a large animal pads through it. After a dozen yards, he begins to sing. I know that song. It's one of Ma's favorites. I watch until I can't see him any more, and as I watch, the air begins to vibrate around me, as if it is purring. I feel myself slipping away, the pain in my side fading, a smell like newly uncurled leaves rising to meet me.

About The Author

For about a dozen years, Dorothy A. Winsor taught technical writing at Iowa State University and served as the editor of the Journal of Business and Technical Communication, but then she decided writing young adult (YA) fantasy was more fun.

The Wind Reader was published by Inspired Quill in fall 2018, followed by *The Wysman*, *The Trickster* and *Glass Girl*. Dorothy's latest title (for now!), *Dragoncraft*, released in 2024.

Her previous novels include *Finders Keepers (2015)* and *Deep as a Tomb (2016)*. Her short stories have appeared in Swords and Sorcery Magazine, Bards and Sages Quarterly, and FrostFire Worlds.

She lives near Chicago with her husband, who engineers tractors, and has one son, the person who first introduced her to the pleasure of reading fantasy. Her deepest secret is that she once wrote over a million words of Lord of the Rings fanfiction.

There But For
The Grace of God

Howard Robinson

S HE RAN THE back of her hand briskly down the outside of her navy-blue jacket, as if brushing away some imaginary piece of thread that had fixed itself to the fabric. Momentarily she caught the slender gold bangle on her wrist on the black button on her jacket. She inhaled deeply, gripping hard onto the black, leather-bound folder that had been handed to her moments earlier.

For someone the media had variously described as focused, icy cold and blindingly convinced of her own righteousness, she felt unusually on edge; insecure, even. Although surrounded by colleagues, this was a moment that had to be navigated alone. She swigged briefly from a plastic water bottle, dabbed the corner of her lips with a paper tissue and placed the bottle on the edge of the table to her right. Her adrenaline was soaring. She knew deep down that this had the potential to be one of the defining moments of her time in office. It wouldn't be universally popular but universal popularity had never been her quest. Making changes, making a difference, dispensing with those who were going to get in the way of her mission; that was how she wanted to be remembered. That was what she wanted the legacy to be.

A young man to her right coughed nervously as if aiming

to clear his throat on a first date.

"Are you ready, Prime Minister?"

She nodded.

An aide opened the door to Number Ten from the inside and a wall of flashes confronted her as she strode through the door and towards the lectern that had been set up in the road outside.

✧   ✧   ✧

GRACE BAPTISTE POURED a drop of oat milk into a floral China mug before carefully measuring and then stirring in a single spoonful of sugar. She helped herself to two chocolate digestive biscuits from the ceramic biscuit barrel she had been given as a Mothers' Day present by her daughter Francine and turned towards the television that was switched on in the corner. She felt guilty for taking the biscuits.

They were an unnecessary indulgence, especially as she had just popped a lasagne into the oven. But she was on her own; there was nobody to chastise her for it.

As she sat in the slightly worn armchair, she focused on the familiar on-screen figure of Athena Allard, Prime Minister and darling of the Conservative right but pariah for almost everybody else. This was not a person of compassion, Grace had always thought, and a showpiece statement timed to hit the evening news bulletins was rarely the precursor of something positive. She twisted the wedding ring on her finger nervously, the texture of her skin evidence of a life of experience and hardship. Athena Allard had never been one of Grace's political heroes. As the daughter of two members of the Windrush generation, each of whom had been threatened with being stripped of their rights as British citizens, Grace regarded her as an enemy living in plain sight. It was something Allard had, at best, not apologised for when Home Secretary, but of which many also thought she covertly approved.

"Good evening, ladies and gentlemen, it's a little chilly out here so I promise to not keep you too long," Allard began.

Grace bit into the first of the biscuits in the hope they might live up to their name and help her digest what was coming next.

"This evening I want to address the scourge of rough sleeping and to set out how we plan to eradicate the problem."

Grace put the biscuit down and concentrated. This was an issue close to her heart. Perhaps there was some empathy within the Prime Minister's sterile soul after all, she thought.

"Recent research has suggested that there could be as many as three hundred and nine thousand people homeless in England, which represents a rise of some fourteen percent – or thirty-eight thousand people – year on year. Many of these people are being housed in temporary accommodation but more than three-thousand people could still be sleeping rough on our streets every night. The fact that our streets have been consumed by tents, sleeping bags and, in some cases, people lying under cardboard boxes, may be a lifestyle choice for them, but I am here to tell you it is no longer acceptable for the rest of us."

Grace held tightly to her tea but was in too much of a state of anger to drink any of it. How could anyone, she thought, demonstrate such a lack of sensitivity to the plight of others, let alone someone who was supposed to be there to lead; to make lives better.

"Tourism is a vital element in our country's economic wellbeing," the Prime Minister continued. "It contributes an estimated two hundred and thirty-seven billion pounds to our economy and as much as fourteen billion pounds in London alone. These much-valued visitors do not want to spend their holidays, their visits to our country, stepping over, walking past or, frankly, even having to countenance people simply so lazy or self-absorbed that they would prefer to sleep on the pavement than get themselves a job and contribute to our society and our economy like everyone else endeavours to do.

"Well, I'm here to tell you it ends now. Although it has long been a crime to sleep rough or beg on our streets, an offence, I would remind you, that carries a fine of up to a thousand pounds, it would seem that this is an insufficient deterrent. We plan to increase those fines up to two-thousand, five hundred pounds with prison terms for those who intend to sleep rough or are likely to cause a nuisance. For this reason, the government will be bringing forward emergency legislation before Parliament not only requiring that all rough sleepers be arrested but to ensure that they will be speedily transferred to a series of initially six holding camps that we will be establishing in more remote areas around the UK. Those transferred to these facilities will be required to work on the land around these camps for third party organisations and businesses, payment for which will be used to offset the cost of their accommodation and subsistence, such that if there is to be any cost to the taxpayer, it will be kept to an absolute minimum.

"Furthermore, I have been advised that local authorities have been spending around one-point-seven billion on temporary accommodation for homeless people over the last year, money that could be better spent improving local services for hard-working families. So, as part of this new legislation, we will ensure that people in temporary accommodation will also be assigned community service work for third party organisations, with the payment they would receive being used to offset the local authority expenditure. Those that refuse will be transferred out of their accommodation and into the rural holding camps.

"Ladies and Gentlemen, I know that some of our opponents in other parties will try and position our move this evening as uncaring. But what it is, is decisive. We are taking steps that will benefit our economy, will benefit the quality of life in our cities and towns and, ultimately, by showing those that have chosen rough sleeping that it is no longer an option, we will be helping them to get their lives back on track. This is the very definition of compassionate conservatism and, together, we will all enjoy the benefits of bringing it to fruition."

Shouted questions could be heard from the media pack in front of her, almost as if they were baying for her blood. It wouldn't have been the first time, she thought. But she wasn't in the mood to fend off lefty liberal questions put by and on behalf of people who had never been nor, if Athena Allard had her way, ever would be in a position of authority with the power to impose their woke agenda on the nation.

✧   ✧   ✧

NINETY MINUTES LATER, with the words of the Prime Minister still circling her mind, Grace Baptiste could still feel the tingling on the roof of her mouth from where she had eaten lasagne that was hotter than she had imagined. Her lips were also a little numb and the left side of her tongue felt tender. That would teach her not to rush – or at least to eat something cooler when she was in a hurry to go out.

"Grace, my dear, how are you? It's always lovely to see you. Are you ready to bring a bit of relief and companionship to people who need it?"

Grace smiled. She knew the compliments she was being paid were the same that she was given every time the church's Help the Homeless crew went out on its mission. But she didn't mind. They made her feel special.

"Well, it's always lovely to see you too Pastor Michael but you don't need to flatter me too much. I enjoy what we do."

"It is God's work, Grace. As it says in Proverbs, Chapter Nineteen, Verse Seventeen if I recall correctly: Whoever is kind to the poor lends to the Lord, and he will reward them for what they have done."

"Amen to that, Pastor."

Grace turned to her right as Pastor Michael moved, not especially effortlessly, towards others in the group, no doubt dispensing the same compliments that he had just given to her. She continued what she was doing: counting rolls that could be handed out with soup to those who wanted, whilst others bagged up pairs of socks, blankets and other items donated through the church. Soon, the crew would be on the move.

It was a cold night with a hint of drizzle in the air as they made their way onto the streets and towards the pavement beneath the bridge near the river, where many of the homeless would choose to sleep for the minimal shelter it provided. Athena Allard's words echoed in her ears. Who would really make this kind of survival their lifestyle choice?

The group huddled beneath sleeping bags, stained with the consequences of their existence, heard them coming and some began to move towards the trestle table that had been set up to serve them something warm. The whole scene reminded her of that Simon and Garfunkel song she loved so much; the one where the singer sought out the places to which the homeless gravitated. She couldn't remember what it was called. The food was welcome, one man had once told her, very welcome and appreciated; but just as important was being remembered, having somebody who saw them, recognised them as human, even gave them an opportunity to laugh or even smile. Many of the faces were familiar – there were nods and smiles as people gratefully accepted what was on offer and spent the moment feeling almost normal again.

Grace noticed one young man who remained seated, his back against the damp interior brick wall of the bridge, leaning against the graffiti. He wore a black beanie hat, the top of his jeans just about visible beneath a once-light grey blanket. She wandered across, stood in front of him and smiled.

"I'm Grace."

The young man – almost still a boy – looked up. There was sadness, fear and exhaustion etched into his face.

"Daniel," he replied.

"Well, Daniel, would you like to come and get something hot to eat?"

"I don't have any money, I'm afraid."

"Nobody is asking you to pay. We just want to give you something. We may have other things that you need too. We come from the church twice a week."

"I'm sorry, but I don't really believe in a God. If he existed, I'm not sure he would allow us to be living like this."

"Well, that's a deep question that we could spend a long time talking through, but better done on a full stomach than an empty one."

Grace held out her hand for him to take.

"You don't have to believe in God for us to help you. And you don't have to believe in God to accept that help. Come, let's get some soup."

Daniel hauled himself to his feet and walked alongside her.

"Do you mind me asking how old you are, Daniel?"

"Nineteen."

"And how long have you been on the streets?"

Grace detected unease.

"You don't have to tell me. I won't be offended. But we might be able to get you more help if we know more about your situation." She could sense him processing the question and weighing up the negatives and the potential benefits of letting the conversation go further.

"I'm coming up to eight months, now."

"That's a long time and in a lot of not very nice weather."

"You get used to it."

"Really?"

"Err... no. You don't"

They both laughed a little.

"So, how come we haven't met before?"

Daniel took the large white cup of steaming soup that was handed to him, and Grace held a white roll in a napkin whilst they found somewhere to sit down.

"This soup's good," he beamed. "It's a long time since I've had something with flavour."

"Well, there's plenty more where that came from, don't you worry."

"I've never been down here before. I didn't know anything about it. I heard some of the guys talking about it when I was south of the river. I didn't want to ask too many questions because, you know, sometimes people can turn on you for no reason, but these guys seemed genuine and told me where to come and when. I thought this morning that I would give it a try and see if what they were saying was true."

"Well, I'm glad you did."

"You and me both," he smiled, dunking the edge of the roll into the soup and then wiping away a little drip that lingered on his chin.

Grace and Daniel sat together, neither feeling the need to speak to be a comfort to each other. Daniel bit into the roll and turned towards his new companion.

"So, how come you are down here? How long have you been doing this?"

"That's a good question," Grace inhaled, trying to give herself time to assess what answer she should give. "I've been coming here and to other places for two or three years now. My husband, Kenneth, passed away just over three years ago. Pancreatic cancer. It was mercifully quick, and he went peacefully but it left me with little to occupy my time. I'm in my early sixties, which my daughter tries to convince me is still young, and being part of this church group has given me new companionship. It hasn't replaced Kenneth, of course. Nothing could do that but I'm not the type of person who wants to just sit in an armchair for the rest of their lives. Kenneth wouldn't have wanted that either. I need to have a purpose. This not only gives me friends, but it has also given me that purpose. I feel like if I can make things even a tiny bit better for somebody else then my day has had purpose."

"That's cool, Grace. Can I call you Grace?"

She reached across, placing her hand around the top of his wrist and squeezed gently.

"Your turn and then we can get you some more to eat."

"I've never really told anyone this," Daniel stared into the distance, determined not to make eye contact.

Grace sat back against the wall, feeling the dampness permeating her top, and watched the growing line of men and women queuing for a small cup of soup and some human interaction. Some were dirty, their hair lank from an inability to shower; others keeping warm beneath torn blankets and well-worn sleeping bags. They were washed by the light from the streetlamps as they stood in line, like undefined characters in an old Lowry painting.

"My stepfather was the reason I left," Daniel began without warning. "I don't think he ever really liked having us around. We always seemed to be in the way."

"We?"

"Me and my sister. He tried at first to like us, I suppose, but the more he drank, the handier he got, if you get my drift."

"That couldn't have been easy."

Daniel laughed an ironic laugh, shaking his head intensely as he did so.

"It's not fun having to constantly look over your shoulder in your own home. I could take the insults, the abuse. I just shut my door, stuck some headphones on and tried to block him out with loud music. But the first time he thumped me, that's when I knew I had to get out. But, as you can see, I didn't really think it through that well."

"And your mum and your sister?"

"I wanted them to come with, for all of us to leave together. But my mum said it was her house and she wasn't leaving it. I think she was in denial, even when I started asking her about the bruises on her arms, she made up some bollocks about falling over in the kitchen. Excuse my language."

"I've heard worse."

"She's probably still in denial. And my sister wouldn't leave unless my mum came with. She's younger, a mummy's girl and, I get it, but I worry about them, then I tell myself I also have to worry about myself, and then I feel bad because I should be protecting them, not running away from them."

"None of this is your fault, you know."

The conversation paused.

"Are you still in contact with your mum and sister? Do they know you are okay?"

He shook his head, despondently.

"I managed to keep my phone working for a few days after I left but then ran out of money. I sent them both texts but didn't get any replies. He's probably checking their messages, so I didn't want to give too much information away. Either that or he's changed their numbers and deleted mine. He probably wouldn't have told them even if he *had* seen my messages. I wouldn't put anything past him."

Grace sighed.

"If you told me their names and gave me a bit more information, we could try and get a message to them, if you wanted me to?"

"Thanks," said Daniel, "but I think that would be a bit too much of a risk for them. I tell myself that one day we will see each other again; that one day we will all be together, having fun and that he will be nowhere on the scene. But for now, as weird as it sounds, I think I'm safer where I am; not that I'm suggesting it's a – what was it that monster Allard said – a *lifestyle choice?*"

"Oh you heard about that, did you?"

Daniel laughed.

"Yeah, some of the guys listened to her on the radio and

were talking about it. I mean, does she really think this is the life we'd choose if we had another option? Maybe she should come and spend the night with us and see for herself how much of a lifestyle choice it is. She wouldn't last an hour. And now she's going to have us arrested, put in prison or ship us off to some concentration camp in the countryside somewhere because we don't look good for tourists. Well, I'm sorry because I know you're a religious lady, but she can go fuck herself."

Now it was Grace's turn to laugh. "I may not have put it the way you just did – but I can't say I disagree, either. Where are you sleeping tonight?"

"I think I'll stay here tonight. The people seem okay; strength in numbers and all that, and I'll just try and keep my head down."

"Promise me you'll come back and see us again when we are here on Thursday night?"

"If the soup is as good again, I'd be an idiot not to."

Grace reached into her pocket to pull out a small white card and a ballpoint pen, which she used to scribble across the back of the card.

"Daniel, this is my mobile number. You can call me whenever you need to. I mean it. I don't want you to feel alone anymore."

Daniel had to hold back tears. "Thank you, Grace. Really, thank you."

✧　✧　✧

"A SUCCESSFUL EVENING everyone," Pastor Michael called out to the group, as they began to pack things into the back of the van for the return journey to the church. "You are all doing God's work."

The group variously smiled or muttered thanks, probably preferring that the dear pastor spent less time thanking them and a little more time helping to load boxes into the back of the van.

"Can I help you with that?"

Grace turned, clutching onto a tea urn that was rusting slightly near the lid. The lead with the plug at the end hung down, swinging back and forth against her leg. She estimated the man in front of her to be in his mid-thirties. He was well dressed, clean shaven and polite. But she was not one to judge anyone in any circumstances.

"That's very kind of you. But we're packing up. I can try and find a roll and some soup if you don't mind waiting a few moments. I'm sure we still have some left."

The man smiled, stifling a chuckle in the process.

"Thank you, but, no, I don't need any soup – not that it didn't smell amazing. I just wanted a chat if I could. My name's Martin. I'm a journalist."

"And what would you want to have a chat about with me?"

Grace handed the tea urn across, feeling her lower back once she had let go and watched as the man lifted into the back of the van, picking the lid up from the pavement after it toppled off in the process. He rested his backside on the floor of the van and smiled at Grace.

"You probably heard the Prime Minister's statement earlier this evening?"

Grace nodded.

"I want to write a piece about it from the point of view of people like you, who come out to help the homeless and, ideally, tell some of their stories too just to rebuff the claims she is trying to make."

"Well, they need to be rebuffed, that's for sure. If she had listened to the young man I was talking to this evening, she would surely have seen that what she has been saying is just divisive nonsense. She just wants to preserve her own position by turning people against people."

"Maybe you could introduce me to him, the young man

you were talking to? Maybe I could speak to the two of you together?"

"We're just ordinary folk. We're not experts on anything. I'm just trying to help and he's just trying to survive."

"And that's what makes your stories so powerful. I think people are a bit fed up with so-called experts. I think it's time for ordinary voices to be heard loud and clear so that we can try and put a stop to all of this before it gets too far down the road."

Grace glanced to her right where she could just make out Daniel's lonely frame, restored to what had become to him a familiar state of isolation. His loneliness pulled at her heart and the notion that this was his choice burned deeply into her soul.

"Give me a moment," she said to Martin.

The three spoke for nearly an hour. Having spent the last eight months doing whatever he needed to do to be anonymous and unseen, Daniel was initially reticent, lest any publicity should be an invitation to those who supported Athena Allard to come and teach him a thing or two. But he believed this Martin, when he said that this would be a start of a brighter future rather than the continuation of a darker present, and even more so when Grace reassured him as well. It was agreed that the locations where he spent his days and nights would go unmentioned and he would only be referred to by his first name. Martin had even offered to give Daniel an alias, but he was finding himself emboldened by the prospect of making a difference, however small, and not just for himself.

The article ran two days later, on the newspaper's front page. Martin had given Daniel a second-hand mobile phone with a pay-as-you-go SIM card inside, which he had topped up to enable the two to stay in contact. The only numbers in the phone were his and Grace's. Daniel kept the phone hidden and on silent, lest anyone should see and fancy their chances of taking it from him. He only checked it when he knew he was on his own. But despite receiving a text message from Martin the night before the story broke, seeing himself on the front page of a national newspaper outside one of the shops nearby was something for which he could never have been prepared. The photograph that Martin had taken that night – reproduced almost as wide as the whole front page – showed Daniel, his face blurred, sitting inside his sleeping bag, the blanket Grace had given him around his shoulders, holding Grace's hand as she stood over him offering him a hot drink, had been designed to pull at every heartstring. The headline provided the punch – *"This Is Nobody's Lifestyle Choice, Daniel tells PM"*.

The interview covered pages two and three as well, telling Daniel's story as much as was possible without giving too much away. Key quotes from the story had been extracted and reproduced in a larger font for emphasis.

"Rather than condemn them as criminals or ship them off to camps, why not open some of the many empty public buildings, give them a home, some support, an opportunity," Grace was quoted as saying. "Why not show them some compassion? But maybe the Prime Minister is devoid of any."

The most impactful part of the article was the part that Daniel had written himself. He had shared with Martin that he had always enjoyed writing and had foolishly hoped one day to write scripts for television or film. And so, Martin had challenged Daniel to write a piece on the phone that he had been given, describing what it felt like to be homeless, to be unseen, and now to be condemned. When the piece arrived on various text messages, it was visceral. And the power moment came at the end when Daniel wrote:

"I don't know the Prime Minister. I've never met her. So, I'm not going to condemn her as many people are. She doesn't understand my existence, my story and the stories of other people who are sleeping under bridges, scraping together coins for food, living in fear of being beaten or spat at, and reliant on the goodness of people like Grace to give us just an inkling of hope. How could she understand that? But if she would like to come out of Downing Street and come and sit with me here, I will happily share my experience with her first-hand."

In that moment, Martin knew he had the silver bullet. They would lay down a challenge to Athena Allard to meet Daniel and Grace. The question was, would she accept?

✧   ✧   ✧

"I'M NOT GOING to be set up like this," the Prime Minister shouted, banging her clenched fist down on the leather desktop. "Just look at the optics. They wheel out this do-gooding, Church-going old lady with the young boy purely to make me look like Cruella DeVille and without any regard for a solution to what is a major problem. So, the answer is no."

If it looks like a duck, quacks like a duck… it's probably a duck, the young aide, standing by the door thought to himself, but neither did he have enough of a death wish to express his view.

"Unfortunately Prime Minister," his boss said, "the more we refuse a meeting or a visit, the more the press are going to demand it. My understanding is that the lady, Grace and the young man, Daniel, are being invited onto several of the daytime television programmes to be the face of the kickback against your… our… proposals. They're not going to let this one go. In fact, we know they are going to come back with an alternative new angle."

Athena Allard had her head in her hands.

"What new angle?"

"We don't know exactly but we believe it's around the use of empty public buildings as referred to in the article to provide homes for homeless people as part of a broader rehabilitation programme. The journalist, Martin Walker, has been touting a few statistics in support of this idea. For example, that local authorities across England, Scotland and Wales have between them enough empty properties to create more than nineteen-and-a-half thousand homes. He also points to a report that *The Observer* ran saying that almost a quarter of a million properties in England have been empty for months."

"And?"

"And, Prime Minister, I think he is planning on using Grace and Daniel as the faces of a campaign led by his newspaper to get you to convert these and other empty public buildings to house rough-sleepers and move them back into education and work. Our view is that it has the potential to gain significant support."

Athena Allard threw her arms into the air.

"The whole country's gone soft," she screamed in exasperation. "People who are not, never will be and don't have the backbone to govern, proposing softly softly approaches to dealing with people who are, frankly, a blight on our society."

It's called compassion, the aide thought to himself. *But you probably wouldn't understand that.*

"Fine," the Prime Minister snapped back after a moment's pause, "cost it. Cost the conversion of these public buildings and all the other woke shit they want to go with it and provide me with a proven case that it's not worth it or, at least, it's way more expensive than our plan and not value for money. And do it fast."

♦　♦　♦

ONE MONTH LATER, and Grace could tell Daniel remained a little uneasy.

"You don't have to worry about your stuff being stolen," she said, reassuringly, reaching across the café table, placing her hand on his. "Pastor Michael has people looking after it. It's perfectly safe."

"I haven't been this far away from it for eight months. If I lose it, I'm done for."

"You're not going to lose it."

Martin pushed the door to the café open, breezing in like a storm brewing, leaning down on the table in front of Grace and Daniel.

"Who wants what?"

They looked at each other and then back towards Martin.

"Are you paying?" Daniel asked.

"Would I have offered if I wasn't?"

The young man perked up. "A full English for me and a mug of tea, please."

"And for you, Grace?"

"I'll go with the same, thank you."

Martin walked back to the counter and placed the order rather than wait for the spaced out waitress to come to them.

"So, you may be wondering why I have asked you to meet me here today," he began loftily.

"This sounds formal," laughed Grace.

Martin tapped his hands on the table to mimic a drum roll.

"I have it on good authority that Athena Allard will announce in the next forty-eight hours that she is ditching her plan to relocate homeless people to detention camps and, thanks to you two – and a little bit to me – will now actively explore opening some empty government buildings and converting them into accommodation and rehabilitation hubs for rough sleepers."

"That's amazing," Grace shouted.

"My sources told me that if she didn't, she was going to face a leadership challenge and so, as we have all suspected, it seems that power rather than principle is more of a motivation for her. Though I'm told, the compromise is that any rough sleeper who refuses accommodation and a place on the rehabilitation programme could still be subject to legal action."

"But this is still going to take ages, isn't it? To convert the buildings?"

"It will take months, for sure, but from little acorns grow mighty trees. You achieved this, Daniel. *You.*"

"Don't get me wrong. I'm grateful for all that you've done, Martin – and you, Grace – but it still means another six months or more on the streets for me. I guess it's like having a carrot dangled in front of your face and then just pulled away when you're close enough to smell it."

Grace took a sip from her tea and encouraged Daniel to do the same.

"Well actually," she began, "about that. There was something I was going to ask you."

Daniel looked up.

"Since my husband died, I've been rattling around in a three-bed house all on my lonesome and I have been thinking for a while that I could use some company. Would you like to move in and use one of my spare rooms as your own? Come and live with me for a while until we get you properly back on your feet?"

"But I can't pay you any rent?"

"Who's asking for rent? It will be helping us both out."

Daniel was shaking his head a little in disbelief.

"Then I'd love to, Grace, though I'm not sure I could ever thank you enough."

"Well, keep shaking your head, young man."

Daniel looked at Martin as if he couldn't take any more.

"You told me when we first met that before you ended up homeless, you had wanted to be a writer. Correct?"

Daniel nodded.

"So the piece you wrote for us as part of the feature was pretty good. Well, very good. Good enough that we thought you might like some paid work experience on the paper doing a bit of writing and reporting. If it works out okay, it could be the start of something longer term."

"That's amazing," exclaimed Grace, her voice welling up a little. "What do you think?"

"What do I think?" beamed Daniel. "I think *yes*."

"Okay," Martin replied. "Get yourself settled at Grace's and then come in and meet the guys at the paper and we can sort out the details. No promises but hopefully it will give you some options. And one more thing."

"Not sure I can take anything else."

"Does the name Katie mean anything to you?"

Grace fixed her stare at Daniel, whose gaze was one of fear, excitement and just raw emotion.

"My sister," he whispered.

Martin nodded.

"She got in touch after the piece ran in the paper. She guessed from the story and what she could see of your picture that it might have been you. She wanted to know if you're okay."

"Is *she* okay?"

"She's fine. And so is your mum. They managed to follow your example and leave your stepfather. They've been living in temporary accommodation. They want to see you."

"Oh my God. I want to see them."

"I'm glad you said that," laughed Martin, glancing at his watch, "they'll be here in half an hour."

Daniel and Grace hugged with a strength neither realised they still had.

About The Author

In his writing, Howard Robinson enjoys taking ordinary people and placing them in extraordinary situations and playing around with the way they would respond. He says it brings out the megalomaniac in him.

Howard's Modern History degree taught him the importance of structure in writing and of exploring language and his long career in PR has given him the opportunity to write on the broadest possible range of subjects.

But essentially, Howard says he writes for himself. He tries to create stories he would enjoy reading, to explore situations and emotions safely within the confines of the page. He aims to create worlds and characters with whom readers can identify and sympathise, which can be seen in both *Micah Seven Five* and *Know Your Own Darkness*, alongside his self-published work, *The Third Republic*.

He lives in London with his wife.

Liminal Voyage

David Wilkinson

O CEAN FELT THE warm water spreading tendrils through her *hair*, before it ran out and pushed away the gelatinous coating laid down by one hundred and twenty years of sleep. The plastic was finally steaming up. Despite a warm *head*, she still felt so cold inside. Cold to the core. Too cold for her metabolism, but a sea of drugs and enzymes was washing around her system, taking care of biochemical processes and keeping her upright. Water at twelve degrees had felt warm when she got into the shower but now it was up to twenty-three. A shape loomed up beyond the steamed-up plastic and Fly's *genitals* pressed up against it where the water had made it clear, wiping back and forth. She banged her *fist* against the inside of the cubicle and he withdrew, squeaking, but she shouted anyway.

"God, Fly. You're such a schlocky child."

"Love pay you, Ocean."

Idiot.

Section 238. Sexual harassment in the work place. Reduced to an insignificant offence in the emergency regulations. Loss of privileges. No privileges to lose any more. Offence thus reduced to just something that is taken.

"How much longer you got?" His *face* pressed up this time but at a spot where the condensation was thick. On the inside of the screen of course, so the view was fuzzy at best.

"Dunno. About an hour? Leave me alone, you pervert." He saw her *fist* coming this time and yanked his *head* back before she connected. "Make it thorough, won't you?" he said. "A full twenty minutes when you get to forty-two."

"You think I can't remember a protocol I was told yesterday?"

"Sure, yesterday."

"Just go and join the others, will you? Leave me be."

"No, Ocean. It will blunt things. Far more dramatic if we walk in together. See their colours as they realise they are so monumentally screwed."

She didn't reply.

He never could leave a silence, and started again. "They're screwed. *We're* screwed. All of us. And the only ones who know it are you, me and Brain."

"And the captain."

"You think? Hey, Brain. Does the captain know me and Ocean have been cooked?"

"Yes, Fly, of course. Although I would characterise it more as a defrost setting."

"No one else?"

"No one else. As soon as Ocean is finished you should both go up to the day cabin. Briefing will start once you're settled. Be safe, though, Ocean. I'll let you know when your core sensor is at forty-two, then you can purge."

Ocean raised her voice over the running water.

"Hey, Brain. Tell Fly to wait somewhere else will you?"

"I do not have that authority, Ocean."

She thought a moment.

"Brain, I want to report Fly for a section two-thirty-eight violation."

Brain hesitated, then said, "Fly, I have reviewed the surveillance record and find that you indeed committed the infringement. You are sentenced to one hour's absence from the reanimation cabin."

Ocean yellowed as she heard him swear and stomp out.

✧   ✧   ✧

BOTH NOW IN ship's overalls, they hesitated outside the door of the day cabin, savouring the anticipation of the stir their arrival would cause. Fly looked serious for once and was standing closer to the door control but not using it. He leaned and whispered into her *ear*.

"It just got real."

"You think if they don't see us we can make it go away?"

"We don't know what *it* is yet. Ocean, you open the door, won't you?"

He stepped back as she reached across and lifted the button cover. Like him, she hesitated at the thought of opening the box and killing the *cat* or worse, making it live. Irritation at being compared to Fly flexed her *finger*. A hum, and the door was open. Every face turned toward them – whipped round by the noise, no doubt. *Mouths* open. Lieutenant Stone with food half way from her plate, spoon stopped in midair. All murmuring one long, low word, "Schloooooock…"

The colours… Fly was right. Green to the red of surprise at the unexpected waking of more crew to the brown of fear and confusion at the import of who they were. Those with bravado forced a transition back through green to neutral and a couple slipped to yellow. She glanced at Fly who had done the same as he marched up to the food bank.

"Hello, chaps! Everything alright? How long have you been up? Schlock, wasn't it cold? Tell me which grub's best, won't you? So hungry after the purging. Wasn't that awful? Nice to have real blood again, don't you think? Mmmm, this smells like undercurrent shrimp. Nothing but the best for us, eh? Shove up, Hill, won't you…?"

Ocean followed him across to the food bank but just filled a beaker with stap and took some clips. The thought of a substantial meal right now turned her *stomach*. Tree made room for her and she seated herself on the bench that encircled the large, communal table. Tree, yellowing, was the first to speak now that Fly was stuffing shrimp paste into his *mouth*.

"It's so nice to see you, Ocean. Give me a touch, will you?"

Ocean *fingered* her face and they cleaved for a moment. It broke the tension for everyone and the questions started. She let Fly answer while looking round the table and feeling lucky to be back amongst them, despite the circumstances.

"No, I don't know why we've been defrosted but isn't it obvious…? Yes the captain knows… No she hasn't spoken to us and Brain hasn't said anything either… There's supposed to be a briefing soon…"

There was enough time for everyone to get more stap before the captain joined them and took a seat. She enquired as to Fly and Ocean's health politely enough despite the importance of the answer. Everyone else was in silence as was to be expected, but fighting not to show colours of impatience. Finally the captain raised her *face* to the ceiling.

"Brain! Brief us please, won't you?"

"Yes, captain. We will take the mission parameters as read. Acceleration phase was uneventful. Hydrogen scooping was as anticipated…"

"Skip ahead please, Brain, won't you?"

"Just decided to start off with good news, captain, but I realise good news is dull. Our full spectrum of telescopes has been directed at the objective the whole time apart from six *hours* in the inversion phase. Resolution has obviously increased over time and we've seen eight planets. The outer four are gas-giants and four inner are rocky. Number three is in the habitable zone, has liquid water and is the source of the oxygen-carbon readings. Oxygen at twenty point nine five percent."

"That's a bit low for us," said Hill but, when irritated

colours were turned on him, rapidly added "But far better than we dared hope. Really. Please Brain, continue won't you?"

"Over the period of our voyage, carbon levels in the atmosphere have risen precipitously."

There was muttering round the table.

"Four and a half years ago in our frame of reference Planet Three became active in the radio wave spectrum. I have converted it to audio for you."

A pulsing sound, not regular but patterned. Ocean looked at everyone reacting with green and red. Tree caught her eye and touched for a moment as she asked Brain, "What does it sound like now?"

Everyone flinched as the mournful beeping was replaced with a loud cacophony, a soup of noise pervading the room and seemingly washing through their minds. It was all of two seconds before it cut to abrupt silence. The captain was on her *feet.*

"Brain! Was that really necessary?"

"I wished to make clear the nature of the problem."

"Did you do anything useful before you woke us up?"

"My progress has been very recent. An increase in signal complexity, I believe, heralded televisualisation but I was unable to deal with its analogue nature. That started around the same time as multiple gamma bursts from the planet's surface."

"Love pay us all…" moaned Honesty, the physicist. Brain continued.

"Digitalisation of the signal finally occurred and deciphering became just a large mathematical problem."

The screens above their heads lit up with images of bipeds jabbering away as only undisputed masters of the universe would.

"So the captain and I thought it would be prudent to awaken Anthropologist Fly and Astrobiologist Ocean."

About The Author

David lives in Ashby de la Zouch, land of Jaffa Cakes, Ivanhoe, and the National Forest. He's a physicist and, after being a research scientist for the Government, he worked for the Institute of Physics. In 2021 he started work at the National Space Centre in Leicester, where he runs the National Space Academy.

It was David's wife who eventually got weary of him talking about all the books he was going to write and told him to get on with it or shut up – buying him a place on a novel writing course for his birthday.

In 2015, his debut novel *We Bleed the Same* was shortlisted for the East Midlands Book Award, which shows the cross-genre appeal of his writing. His second novel, *Under The Shell*, is a sci-fi noir set in the same universe but is a stand-alone novel.

David fills his time outside of authoring and his job with handling two 18+ offspring, cooking a lot, walking three tiny dogs, and continuing a four-year mission to visit all 76 cities in the UK.

Seven Days to Save Bakatam

Daniel Stride

T O SING OF Bakatam-that-is-gone is to sing of a wonder of the Ancient World. For though none now walk its ways, and its houses stand sad and silent, and its stone walls and towers crumble into dust, things were otherwise in the days of yore, when the morning-dews of Spring yet lay upon the face of the Earth and even Viiminia-across-the-Sea was young.

Each feast day, the high and silvered domes of Bakatam's glorious temples rang with the prayers of the people, and the airs reeked with smoke from burnt-offerings upon altars – oxen kept for purpose by the priests, or as some tales tell it, offerings yet more rare and dreadful, the sacrifice of enemies captured in bloody battle.

Statues of gods and rulers, sculpted and painted, glared with marble eyes upon the streets and squares of the city, where poets and philosophers gathered over amber wines to debate the hidden meanings of beauty. In the shadows of Bakatam's libraries, scholars with palsied hands trembled at texts long-forgotten, while down upon the docks and quays, merchants traded spices and grain, and vendors proffered honeyed treats to visitors and children. Thus the merchants of Bakatam grew prosperous, and the seagulls fat.

If other ports rose in time to become larger and richer, with grander fleets and more plentiful sailors, with fiercer land-armies and brighter swords, it mattered little. No after-comer rivalled the awe of venerable Bakatam, the first jewel of the Western Illuvian Sea.

Perched upon the tip of a peninsula, the city was protected on three sides by the waves. Assault required mastery of the sea, and for many centuries, none might rival the skill and cunning of Bakatam's naval commanders. Folk of other lands whispered too of strange winds, and of sudden swells, that arose in roaring wrath as if from the whims of the gods, and then promptly departed once hostile ships lay wrecked upon the teeth of nearby reefs.

The fourth side, that of the peninsula, was guarded also. But rather than the sea, here a wall stood, sheer and stern, a proud redoubt that repelled all comers. Blood was often spilled before this land-wall, as hungry lords of other cities sought to claim Bakatam's treasures for themselves.

Impregnable by sea, and mighty by land, Bakatam endured. Oft outnumbered, the defenders of the city always emerged victorious. Foiled in their dreams of conquest, the invaders would withdraw, seeking an easier foe.

And so it remained for countless long years.

✧ ✧ ✧

"I REMIND YOU of our treaty."

His face fierce, his beard black and braided in the fashion of his people, the envoy trod the floor of the King of Bakatam's chambers. This was the Duke of Enlomim's younger brother, and he had arrived in the city only yesterday, bearing terrible news from the north.

A vast host of Kruvish swept down from the mountain passes, towards Enlomim, burning and pillaging in their wake. The Kruvish had spent generations warring among themselves, but they now united beneath a single savage leader, and were overwhelming all resistance. The Duke sought aid against this threat, and thus he reached out to Bakatam.

The King rubbed his own sparse beard. A young man, he was but two years upon the throne, and untested in martial combat. Every day, he felt the shades of his father and grandfather scorning him, even as he sought to prove himself worthy of their legacy.

"Bakatam has forgotten nothing," he said. "We shall eagerly assist Enlomin against the Kruvish."

The Queen – three months pregnant – looked up from her window-side chair. She read a book of ancient poetry, and the sun warmed her face.

"Bakatam has always stood firm behind its walls," she said. "In defence we are strongest, as foes break like waters upon a rock."

"Yes," said the King. "But to retreat like a tortoise into its shell would dishonour the city. And who would march to defend us, if we do not march to the side of others?"

"Bakatam has never fallen."

"Even so, since the time of my father, Bakatam has had a treaty with Enlomin and her neighbours. I myself shall ride out, so that all men shall know this city keeps its word."

"You endanger yourself, and the life of our child."

The King smiled.

"One day, our child shall understand."

✧   ✧   ✧

The Queen and the High Priest stood together upon Bakatam's walls, and watched the army depart along the dusty peninsula road. Though wars were no new thing, the scale of the force was vaster than any seen for long years. The King sought to impress his allies with his fidelity to their cause.

Indeed, the Queen wondered if the hoariest greybeard in

the city could remember such a sight – row upon row of spearmen, the sun glinting upon the wrought steel of their helmets. Horsemen too, and archers, and the lords of Bakatam in their full and glorious might. All marched through the Great Gate, and away to the battle before Enlomin.

Truly, the King carried off the very flower of Bakatam's youth, along with the great bulk of the city's martial strength.

"I fear for them," said the Queen. "What of the omens? What word from the gods?"

The High Priest did not take his eyes off the marching soldiery.

"The omens are strange, my Queen. They speak indeed of the Kruvish being finally turned back, amid the great heroism of Bakatam. The foe shall not breach our city's defences, and songs shall be sung for generations to come. And yet..."

"And yet?"

"The omens speak of you, my Queen. And not our lord, the King. I cannot fathom it, though I daresay all shall reveal itself in time."

The Queen did not interrogate the High Priest further. A cloud of dread passed over her heart, and though the day was warm, she shivered.

✧   ✧   ✧

SEVEN DAYS LATER, a storm descended upon Bakatam, the worst in memory. The people of the city saw great forks of lightning in the sky, like so many columns of white fire, and they heard the hollow boom of thunder. Waves like snow-topped mountains crashed upon the sea-cliffs. Rain and hail pelted roofs and crops. Ships broke loose from their moorings amid the wildness of the winds, and so sank with crew and cargo. Safe within their temples, even the priests wondered what had so stirred the gods to wrath.

The Queen sat beside the hearth, and gave such orders as she could. But her thoughts remained on the High Priest's words, and the fate of her husband.

✧   ✧   ✧

"My Queen," said the grey-bearded Chamberlain. "We have tidings from the battle at Enlomin."

The Queen blinked weary eyes. Salvaging Bakatam from the storm had drained her. Bread and meat rationing might be expected. But homeless folk still lurked in archways, and destitute merchants still screamed of ruin, or else threw themselves from cliffs into the sea... this was more than she had imagined. She had decreed special sacrifices at the temples, and gifted silver candlesticks towards the rebuilding of the ships, but it seemed so little. She still felt so utterly helpless.

Now, at last, the moment had come...

"What news?"

The Chamberlain gestured mournfully.

A gaunt and hollow-eyed man, his beard stained with dark blood, hobbled into the room. Still clad in breastplate and battered helmet, he was flanked by two Palace Guards.

The soldier went to kneel, but such was his weakness, he collapsed prone upon the stone floor.

"My Queen," he groaned.

The Queen rose from her hearthside seat.

"Where is my husband? Where is the army?"

"Your husband is dead." A soft chuckle. "I am the army."

"You?"

"All but me slaughtered... gone."

The Chamberlain and the Queen looked at each other. Blood had drained from both their faces.

✧   ✧   ✧

AS THE SUN set upon Bakatam, word spread to temple and library, alley and tavern, and down to the storm-wrecked docks: the King lay dead, along with all the great lords, and even his entire army. Few remained within the city walls who had not lost a husband, a brother, a father, or a son. Tears fell like rain, and the agonised cries of those left behind swept through the streets in a baleful music. The Queen was not the only widow to offer desperate candlelit prayers to the gods that night.

But there were whispers too, gathering force in the days that followed – whisperings only partly tinged with grief and despair. Increasingly, they rang with fear and horror, and anticipation of what was to come. Panicked refugees, stained with dirt and dust, brought further word from the war. Tales of a dreadful Sack, of priest blood spilt upon holy places, and of smoke-clouds that blotted out the very sun.

For the Kruvish – not content with the mere Sack of Enlomin, and the butchering of its people – were now marching south, in great numbers. The head of the defeated Duke, so rumour went, adorned a spike at the front of the procession. Or perhaps his corpse hung upon a rope from his own tower, as sport for crows and archers. Or maybe his body had been roasted upon a spit, and devoured in a rancorous cannibal feast, as was often the way with the cruel Kruvish of the mountains.

But though details differed, the accounts all agreed on one thing. The Kruvish came for the final prize, that which had never been attained by any foreign force.

They came for Bakatam.

✧   ✧   ✧

"EVEN SO," SAID the Chamberlain the next morning. "Bakatam's walls yet stand."

The Queen stared northwards, out the window. From the

paved square before the palace, down over the tree-lined streets, towards the Great Gate. Gloomy the city's mood might be, yet there was still hope. The Kruvish possessed no navy, and that land-wall guarding access from the peninsula… that land-wall had never been breached.

"Few are left to man the defences," said the Queen.

"The Palace Guards, the Watchmen, and the civilian militia," said the Chamberlain. "Whatever old men and shepherd-boys we can find. We shall give bows to those who can shoot, and spears to those who cannot. Why, I myself shall stand alongside them."

It was no idle pledge. He had donned both breastplate and helmet. A sword hung at his hip, though the Queen wondered when he had last wielded it in earnest. The Chamberlain was no military man, and even in his youth had preferred the quiet of paperwork and administration to the danger of the campaign or the sea.

"The women of the city shall pray within the temples, that we might yet regain the favour of the gods," she said. "I myself already lead the prayers."

"As you say, my Queen. For the gods have guided our city through greater perils than this. Perhaps they shall heed your supplications, and drive the Kruvish away. Has the High Priest not declared the goodness of the omens? That your deeds shall bring us victory worthy of song?"

Before the Queen could answer, the ground shook beneath her feet. A sudden, violent jolt. Candlesticks swayed, then tumbled off shelves, and rattled onto the floor.

"Earthquake!" yelped the Chamberlain. He shoved her down, and swatted away a falling silver plate.

The Queen crawled beneath a table. The Chamberlain swiftly joined her.

The tremor ran on and on, rolling and terrible. Bakatam was no stranger to earthquakes, and its people yet remembered the one twelve years ago, which had damaged the Great

Temple's silvered dome and toppled one seaside tavern. But to be caught in such an event now… the Queen prayed for the abatement of divine fury.

At last, the ground grew still again.

"We must flee," said the Chamberlain. "The palace is not safe."

"To the courtyard," said the Queen. "And hurry."

✧   ✧   ✧

DOWN THE WINDING stairs of the Palace, they dashed. Signs of destruction lay strewn everywhere – overturned statues, broken busts, cracked walls. About them, the Palace Guards were in a ferment, running this way and that, like a hive of startled bees. One of them – a man who served the midnight patrol – had clearly been shaken from his bed, and ran through the corridors stark naked and red-cheeked. But at least they had the courtesy to bow before their ruler, and as the Queen ran onwards, the Palace servants and officials gathered about her in a protective escort.

"Follow me," the Queen called.

Her people obeyed. They had little choice.

✧   ✧   ✧

THE MORNING SUN shone bright and clear upon Bakatam, but that was chill comfort indeed. That which the storm had weakened, the earthquake had riven and destroyed. Whole houses now stood as piles of rubble, their people lost and homeless. One of the temple domes had collapsed. The priests outside wailed in mourning.

The Queen walked the streets, inspecting the damage in the company of the Chamberlain and Palace Guard. Her heart sank. Bakatam would require months of labour to repair itself, and nigh-all the silver in the royal treasury.

But Bakatam did not have months. If reports were true, it had barely seven days, ere the Kruvish arrived.

"Show me the land-wall," she said to the Chamberlain. "Let us see whether it still stands."

Even as the Queen spoke, she knew the truth.

✧   ✧   ✧

IT WAS AS she dreaded.

The land-wall, Bakatam's shield, had crumbled amid the fury of the earthquake, and toppled in numerous places. The Great Gate still stood, but elsewhere the devastation was palpable. Square stones lay scattered along the width of the narrow peninsula. The Queen prodded one fallen stone with her foot. The Kruvish, when they arrived, would find an unprotected city, with neither wall nor garrison worthy of the name.

"Have our very gods forsaken us?" she murmured. "What blasphemies have I committed, that this might come to pass in my time?"

She felt a tug at her sleeve. The Chamberlain.

"We cannot repair the land-wall," he said. Quietly, so only she heard. "We must take ship to the islands, and return when the Kruvish have gone."

She eyed his breastplate and helmet.

"I thought you would stand in desperate defence against the foe."

"I would stand defence, my Queen, until the bitter end, if only the wall yet stood. Alas, my hope died with it… and I see now our only chance is to flee."

"You take the path of cowards," she said.

"It is the path of prudence. Else, we shall be cut down by the invaders. Better something of the city survives, that we might rebuild in time."

The Queen shook her head.

"I shall not abandon my people."

"Then you and your unborn child shall die with them, and Bakatam shall perish utterly."

"No," she said. "For the High Priest spoke of omens. I see now what I must do."

She pulled away, and marched across the road, to a gap in the wall. Throngs of folk stood about, gazing at the destruction. Watchmen too, and her loyal Guard.

"People of Bakatam," she called. "Heed your Queen!"

At once, the murmurings ceased. All eyes were upon her. Yet more people emerged from the shadows to hear her words.

"Even now, the Kruvish come to despoil your city. But we shall not let them. No, we shall endure."

"We have lost our wall," someone called back.

"Then we shall rebuild," said the Queen.

Silence. None could believe it. Perhaps they deemed her mad with grief. But the Queen went on.

"We have seven days and nights, and the strength of a city. We have the stone. We shall make fresh mortar from sand and lime. All we need is the will to piece the wall back together."

"We cannot work without food and rest," called the crowd.

The Queen smiled.

"I have talked with my honourable Chamberlain. He shall take responsibility for organising bread and shelter. Until the wall is complete, all food in Bakatam – including that from the royal kitchens and warehouses – shall be divided in accordance with strict need. Anyone caught cheating shall face summary execution."

Already, the grey-bearded Chamberlain was spluttering. But he dared not contradict his Queen.

"Stop," called another voice.

Another man pushed his way through the throng. Too old for the army, this one was solidly-built. His red face was framed by a shock of white hair. The Queen recognised him as the Guildmaster of Bakatam's stone-masons.

"My Queen," he said. "You cannot permit non-masons to work upon the wall. It would be unthinkable…"

"Then you and your guild shall oversee them. You must appreciate the urgency of the situation."

"I shall oversee no-one, save my own guild-men. We have a charter."

"Is that your final word?"

"It is, my Queen."

"Then hear mine. I too have a charter. Bakatam and its people shall be protected from foes, so long as I draw breath. Guards… bring me this man's head."

The Guildmaster's red face flushed even redder, as the Palace Guards seized him and led him away.

"No," he wailed. "You cannot do this…"

The Queen sighed.

"Now," she told the crowd. "Go spread the news. The stone-masons guild – under a new Guildmaster – shall oversee the rebuilding, and issue directions. The rest of you… remove these fallen stones, and pile them. The children of the city, too young for heavy labour, shall fetch seashells from the shore, as a fresh source of lime. The potters shall oversee the kilns. Night and day, Bakatam shall work upon the wall."

"My Queen," said the Chamberlain.

"Yes?"

"I shall need assistance with the city's food provision. Emergency shelter too, for those rendered homeless by the earthquake."

Loyalty had clearly steadied the man's nerves. He no longer thought of flight.

"Appoint whomever you need," she said. "Save that labour on the wall cannot be compromised. As for shelter… perhaps the army barracks retains tents, left behind by my husband?"

The Chamberlain bowed.

"I shall do as you instruct," he said.

✦ ✦ ✦

TALES OF THE Kruvish banished all hesitancy from the folk of Bakatam. They knew they must build or die, and the words of the High Priest were repeated from every corner and in every heart. Truly, the city lived in a fabled time, and clung to desperate hope, even as many an old man still wept at the loss of his house and his son.

The new Guildmaster of the stone-masons raised none of the objections of the old, and soon the labour of many cleared the rubble from the site, allowing construction to begin. Under the oversight of the masons, sacks of lime were carried from cellars, and thence mixed with sand to render mortar. Stones were laid back in place, level by level, while the city carpenters and ropers constructed scaffolding as needed.

But the existing lime was supplemented by another steady supply. The children of the city collected buckets of seashells, to their own great delight, to feed the fiery hunger of the lime kilns. In years after, there arose the folk-tradition that shells upon the shore banished the terror of the north.

Other tales might be told of those seven days. The High Priest prayed before the altar of the Great Temple, until his knees deadened and his voice grew hoarse. His own servants had to drag him away, and give him water, ere he collapsed. The Chamberlain erected relief tents throughout open spaces, and though none ate well, none starved. The Queen herself served savoury fish-stew to her people, and ate as they ate, from plain wooden bowls.

And each starry night – for the gods in pity of Bakatam had banished the clouds from the sky in those desperate times – the Queen donned her white woollen cloak, and strode down with her Guards to inspect the work. Torchlight and campfires burned at all hours, casting the wall in an eerie glow, but enough to enable continued construction. When called upon to carry firewood, the Queen took it upon herself to obey, pregnant though she was, even as her people obeyed. Little by little, the land-wall rose anew, for everyone feared the imminent arrival of the Kruvish.

But should anyone lag, or complain of the heavy labour, there was another and just as deadly warning. For nearby, a wooden spike had been driven into the soft ground. Upon it sat the head of the old Guildmaster of the stone-masons.

His red face watched the construction with lifeless eyes.

✧　　✧　　✧

ON THE MORNING of the seventh day, a cloud of dust arose upon the peninsula. A host of armed men, their steel glinting in the sun, rode towards the walls of Bakatam. Numerous as stars in the sky, and deadlier than any viper, this force had ravaged all the lands in its path.

The Warlord of Kruvish, all-conquering Devourer of the World, had come to claim what was his. The jewel of cities that had hitherto evaded all foes.

And yet, as he came within sight of the city, the Warlord's heart failed him. Taking Enlomin had been child's play, once the Kruvish had lured their foes into the open, for its walls were weak and small. The Warlord had heard stories of Bakatam, and scoffed, thinking this merely the bragging of a people both weak and cowardly. He had cut through its foolish King easily enough, those soft lords like lambs to the slaughter. But that had been the King of Bakatam and not the city behind him. Gazing upon the land-wall, high and strong, patrolled by guards in gleaming armour, the Warlord wondered if he had met his match.

Had the earth not shaken but days earlier, sending towers tumbling to the ground? Bakatam's walls had somehow endured even that. Accursed giants must have built this place long ago. But to retreat... his own men would mock his weakness, and throw his carcass to the crows. Thus it had always been among his oft-divided people.

The Warlord halted before the wall, just out of arrow-range. He unfurled a flag of parley. Let him see what the folk of Bakatam might offer.

Trumpets rang, and the Gate opened. Out rode a single man in breastplate and helm. His beard was long and grey, and he showed no fear.

"You have come to treat with the city of Bakatam?" he called.

"We have," replied the Warlord. "Come hither, and let us discuss terms."

❖   ❖   ❖

THE CHAMBERLAIN OF Bakatam was no fighter, as he himself would admit. He had considered the Queen's plan utter madness. Yet day by day, he had watched the rebuilding of the land-wall, and seen the spirit rising within the city – hope in the face of disaster. It had warmed his old heart. And so in similar spirit, he had volunteered to negotiate with the dread Kruvish... perhaps he might yet redeem himself.

Now he sat, weaponless, in the tent of the most terrifying man on the continent. A goblet of good wine in his hand, he listened as the Warlord described his conquests, and how the Kruvish punished any stubborn resistance.

When it came his own turn to speak, the Chamberlain smiled.

"My lord," he said. "Bakatam's mighty walls have been assailed by stronger powers than yours. I myself have seen it. For think not that when you slew our King, that you cut the beating and bloodied heart from our city. We shall resist you, standing strong even as you wilt before our Gate. We command the seas, and you do not – we have a shortage neither of food nor of those willing to fight for their home. And yet, valour speaks to valour… we shall gift you one thousand pounds of silver to depart. A prize greater than any hitherto awarded by the people of Bakatam. What say you?"

"Five thousand pounds," said the Warlord. "And think not that I cannot raze your city to the ground, should you play me false."

"Even the gods could not raze Bakatam, try though they might," said the Chamberlain. "And though we shall not play you false, you stand upon a peninsula, with no ships. Should the folk behind march against you, and take your army in the rear, the Kruvish would be trapped like a rat in a bottle. Three thousand pounds."

"Four thousand pounds."

"Three and a half thousand."

The Warlord lifted his goblet in a toast, and drained it.

"Verily," he said. "Tell your people they have a deal."

✧　✧　✧

THE TEMPLES MELTED down their precious adornments, and the royal treasury was opened. Three and a half thousand pounds of silver were duly gifted to the Warlord, and the Kruvish carried the booty away in great oxen-pulled wagons. But as the people of Bakatam looked out from their earthquake-ridden city, and saw the departing enemy, a grim flutter of pride ran through the heart of Queen and commoner alike.

They had lost so much, and yet they had kept hoping. Their mighty city had once again endured, and all through the strength and bonds of its people.

About The Author

Daniel Stride (also known as Dan) is the author of *Wise Phuul* and a long-time fantasy reader and all-round geek, having fallen in love with The Lord of the Rings aged nine (he still thinks The Silmarillion is the best book ever written).

He spent far too long at University, where he accumulated multiple degrees in-between lobbying politicians and fighting for doomed causes. But he wasn't really a career student – honest – he even had a respectable nine years working for the local newspaper. And now he's a qualified lawyer and security guard…

Apart from reading, writing, and teaching himself foreign languages, he's a member of the Society for Creative Anachronism, with a taste for reconstructing medieval skaldic verse. His only true weakness is chocolate. And cats. But not chocolate cats, because the fur would get all sticky.

Dan lives in Dunedin, New Zealand. He is currently working on increasing his number of short story publications, having recently completed his second novel, *Old Phuul.*

One Who Bears
A Tree Upon Her Back

EA Mylonas

_v3.2

A GLIMMER AND a haze vibrated along the line that separated sky from earth, and an iris split the air, peeling back the folds of that universe.

Out stepped humanity.

Small groups carrying their belongings; whatever they could grab as they ran out of their houses. Carried bundles of clothes, carried packs with food, carried desperation the same way they carried their family portraits, tied hard to their backs.

Ash held baby closer to his chest, protecting it from the dust kicked into the air by the group.

"Another Earth," he sniffed through his nose slits.

"Might be the one," Palm said, stepping into this new universe behind him.

"Hoping is free," Ash replied, completing their little ritual.

They looked up ahead at the border checkpoint standing lonely in the featureless salt desert. A simple shack made from what looked like corrugated iron, dull, grey, with two guards there staring at each other. Nervousness, Ash and Palm had found out, announced itself easily. Nervousness always looked the same on a human face, regardless of how humans had evolved on that Earth, or how alien their features appeared. Apparently, so did disgust, and fear, but also welcoming.

"Let's set up," Palm said and smiled.

Humanity on this world was terrestrial. A blessing. Ash hated breathing water, but, most importantly, because they came from a terrestrial humanity it was easier for them to take on the local human form.

Ash and Palm sat cross-legged on the salt surface, shielding their eyes from the reflection, letting the others pass them by. Took another look at the guards, just to be sure they understood what they were aiming for. Details didn't matter much. They'd fine-tune. As long as they looked close enough to how humanity appeared on this Earth, they had chances of being allowed to stay.

And If Ash and Palm, the only shapeshifters of the group, were allowed to stay, they could advocate for everyone else too, all those other humans from those other strange Earths that had joined them.

Ash's fingertips vibrated. Imperceptibly at first, then faster, until they became a blur. The vibration spread to the rest of his body. Finger by finger and limb by limb, he shed the form he carried from the previous Earth in a haze of particles. The purple mane fell off, the thick horns turned to dust. The double-slits on his eyes fused into one.

When he thought he was done with the transformation, he looked at Palm who was now a head taller than him.

"If you're going to be bigger than me, you're carrying baby."

His own original form had stopped mattering to him a long time ago. Once in a while, he'd reach into his pack and retrieve a picture of him and Palm before baby, and the person that stared back at him triggered a poor echo of a memory in his synapses. He knew that person was him, but did not *feel* anything, not anymore. Didn't matter.

As Palm always said, what mattered was the here, the now.

What mattered was survival. Getting ahead of the Cancer that ate up their world and finding a quiet corner on an Earth so far away that it would never reach them.

Palm stared at her hands. Elongated fingers, all twelve of them with stiletto nails at their tips. Ash guessed they had evolved to spear food hiding in tiny holes. That would be useful to know if they were allowed to stay.

"How do I look?" Palm asked.

"Glorious," Ash replied. Baby, unable to shapeshift yet, unable to comprehend yet, looked startled from one to the other. "Still us, buddy," Palm said and kissed baby on the forehead. "Still us, always us."

A backwards glance through the iris they had stepped through at the Earth they were leaving behind. Ash thought that had been the one.

The one where they'd manage to settle down, finally truly settle down, and rebuild their lives.

The one where baby would grow up.

The one that would become their safety.

Messages from the surrounding universes told them the Cancer had picked up their trail. Was coming for them.

"Queue up for processing," one of the border patrol guards yelled. "Queue up." Next to him, his much larger partner wrung her hands.

_v3.3

THE ONE THAT mostly chose a male form called himself Ash. The one that mostly chose to go by a female form called herself Palm.

After running through a few worlds, they'd noticed that ash and palm trees appeared on every single iteration of Earth. For reasons no one could understand, Earths had always had ashes, had always had palms. Only the names of those trees sounded different depending on how language had evolved there.

And so it became a simple choice ("pragmatic", Palm called it) to shed their old names. Take on new identities. Make it easier for border patrols to process them.

"How do you call Ash in this world?" he asked this new guard on this new Earth. "How do you call Palm? Those are our names."

Their old names, unpronounceable, they had discarded somewhere during their exodus, together with anything that weighed them down.

Like beloved books.

Like his mother's wooden chest and the guitar of Palm's brother.

Like anything they could not use on their long trip to safety.

Ash remembered his given name, and Palm's. He knew that if he concentrated, he'd probably remember their family names too. But he preferred not to.

The baby, they had not named. They wanted to wait until they had settled somewhere, the plan being that they would give it a local tree name, unique to that world. Easier to integrate. Easier to be accepted.

On some nights, Palm joked the baby's name was No-Name. On some nights, Ash muttered that, at the rate they had to give up Earths, the baby's name would forever remain Baby.

He told as much to this guard. This guard, with his hairless body and bug eyes and ten fingers, five on each hand.

"What happened to the previous Earth? Why didn't you stay there?" the guard asked.

"The Cancer."

"The Cancer is there?"

"Yes."

"On our doorstep?"

"Yes."

The guard stared into empty space before waving them through.

_v3.4

Cancer.

Because what other name do you give to the madness of your own body attacking itself? What other name do you give to a disease that spreads until it eats its way into oblivion? What else?

The universe was a living organism, that's what scripture said. With an unknowing mind of its own and incomprehensible will, if a thing like the universe could be imagined wanting anything.

Palm thought this was religious nonsense, fairy tales for primitive people. So did Ash, for a time.

But when their universe started eating itself.

But when stars ripped to subatomic shreds.

But when the night sky turned blackest black and the laws of nature wilted and rotted away.

But when they crossed that first gate into another version of Earth and, against their judgment, looked back to see their world disintegrating into the void.

A dead universe. Cold.

They and others jumped to another Earth, one where humanity could not quite shapeshift like they could. On this new Earth, humans entered cocoons when life became too much to handle and molted into someone else.

Not quite shapeshifters, then. But a sort of kinship did exist. Humans of this Earth accepted them and made a place in their world for them. Until the Cancer found a way through.

They found a gate and moved to another Earth, and another, and another. And did not stop moving.

With time, those that made the first jump with them went

onto their separate paths. Others joined them. And their group grew and shrunk and grew again. Now a pack, now a crowd, always a company.

Ash had heard the name Cancer in a different context as well. Hurled at him and Palm and baby and the others too. Calling the victim after the disease, because they too spread far and wide, trying to stay alive, trying to stay one step ahead. Unfair comparison.

On some Earths, the locals thought the group carried the Cancer with them, or that the Cancer followed them across universes or that they were hexed and somehow responsible for their world's fate, bearing the stigma of a curse.

"Do you think they might be right?" Ash asked Palm as they huddled in their tent for the night.

But Palm gave him a dirty look that silenced him.

"I'm not going to let this nonsense worm its way into my brain. And neither should you." Then, as if regretting her harshness, "I need you to not let this sort of talk mess with you. I need you to stay focused on the goal. I need you."

"And what is the goal?"

Palm stared away and muttered under her breath something that sounded like "survival".

_v3.5

"IT DOESN'T MAKE a whole lot of sense," Ash shook his head while they waited in a queue to be processed. This Earth, with an oxygen-rich atmosphere. With humans that they had to crane their necks to look in the eyes. "If one were to calculate the odds of humanity evolving through extinction level events and ice ages and competition and predators and just plain bad luck… It's almost as if there's a need for this species."

Palm looked ahead at the processing station, at the giant who examined the refugees, and her skin changed hue, turned into an anxious shade of purple that startled baby in the carrier strapped to her back. "Mmm," she said.

Most of their attention was on a small-statured woman and the tree strapped to her back. Had joined their group several Earths back. A gardener. Her only belongings were a few clothes in a pack and the tree that she carried in a burlap sack filled with soil. A tree whose never-ending supply of red fruit with their crown-like calyxes helped the group survive when they couldn't find food or no one would give them any.

"Do you think there's a world without humanity?"

"Don't know."

"It's as if humanity is this universal constant at the heart of an equation, like a familiar tune that plays across universes."

"Okay."

"Are you even paying attention?"

"The guard looks angry. I wish we had the mass to shapeshift into their size."

"My point is, it's almost as if the universe *needs* humanity."

"The universe doesn't need anything." She whistled to the baby, soothing it.

"An instinct, then. A natural reaction to existing."

"What?"

"What if the universe needs humanity to study itself? The way a brain studies itself through the science of medicine? Maybe the universe needs *us* to figure out the Cancer."

"I don't think it works that way."

"How can you prove it doesn't work that way? It's in the scriptures."

But Palm wasn't listening to him anymore. Palm had stepped out of the queue and was marching towards the guard, yelling and throwing her hands in the air as the giant's hands curled into fists and tried to snatch the tree away from the old woman, her people, *their* people.

"Maybe the universe is scared," Ash whispered as he ran after her and baby.

_v3.6

LANGUAGE CHANGED. THOUGH everyone understood "danger". Everyone understood "help me". And they, Ash and Palm, in turn understood "no" and "go back to where you came from".

Ash was better at figuring out how language worked.

"Are you carrying with you anything we should know about?"

Different Earth. Same questions. Easy to pick up a language when the words repeat.

"Gold."

Gold had a name, gold was a *thing* on most Earths. The possibility hadn't even crossed their minds, but the day a merchant pointed at Ash's rings and asked for them as payment for food, they knew.

"Uhm, cigarettes."

Because they made for good conversation starters. Because border guards were bored and twitchy, because they saw kindness as often as a solar eclipse and offering them cigarettes was a sure-fire way to soften their scowls. Because inhaling toxins for pleasure was as common in humanity as bipedalism.

"Bit of soil."

Taken from their garden, locked in a vial on a string around his neck. Did not weigh much/held the weight of a universe.

"Do you carry alcohol?"

"What?"

"Fermented fruit juice, fermented grain juice."

"Ah. No."

"Anything else?"

"Stories."

And stories. Stories made for good currency. Tell a story and someone might offer you a drink or even food if they could spare it.

Stories of that world where humanity descended from birds.

Of that world which had no language but only pheromones and displays of color.

Of that world where the oceans covered the entire planet.

A lot of things changed. A lot more stayed the same. Even across the universes, even across dimensions.

"Excuse me? Stories?" Quills vibrated with hard-to-mask hostility.

"Sorry. Joke only. On the road for days, tired. Talking nonsense."

"This is a border check and not answering my questions is a criminal offence. Do you understand? One that carries a prison sentence. So, I'm going to need you to reframe the way you answer."

"Understand. Tired. Won't happen again."

Dignity, Ash would have wanted to add. Dignity.

_V3.7

UNEXPECTED AT FIRST. Every version of Earth had its own unique smell.

"That doesn't make sense," Palm said when Ash brought it up as they huddled in their tent. "Earth is a big place. Every Earth is, and there's plenty of places in each of them and I'm sure there's plenty of smells, too."

"No. I mean, I understand what you're saying. But every Earth does have a smell of its own. Like a bass note that rumbles beneath a song's harmony. It's there. Beneath all the other smells, it's there. I can't be the only one who's noticed."

"You're the only one who's noticed."

"In the beginning, I thought I was smelling local plants. But I think I'm picking up the fundamental differences between the worlds. Strawberries and faith. Salt water and absurdity."

"You know what I'm about to ask."

"What does this world smell like?"

"Mmm."

Ash concentrated and he breathed deeply through the slits at the base of his beak.

"Not good."

"It doesn't smell good. You're sure it's not baby you're smelling?"

"I'm sure. I've been smelling baby for the last two hours."

"Well, it's your turn to change it."

"You could have said something."

"Me? My nostrils got burned out a few Earths back. I can't smell anything. What scent do we have?"

"Who? Us three?"

"No. Us. All of us."

Ash focused for a second. Looked outside their tent at humanity. A group stared up at the night sky, at low-flying leviathans floating over the camp, communicating with each other in low rumbling notes. He noted their postures, their features. After a while, their belongings, their clothes, even their skins took on a certain patina from the dust of a dozen worlds.

Ash smiled.

_v3.8

ON THE ROAD, though destination eluded them.

This Earth was sparse.

They were allowed to stay, allowed to roam. Allowed to settle, and they would, as soon as they found a suitable place.

When dusk came, the tents went up. As Palm slept, Ash took baby for a walk between the maze of burlap and plastic and shells and carapaces. And he talked to people. Using the pidgin words they had in common and making up new ones as he needed them, adding to a vocabulary of necessity, lexicon of the displaced.

Dis-place. Un-place. No-place.

None of them had a place in this world or any world, but on the road with each other.

Of the thirteen that had been in their group, only Ash and Palm and baby remained. The others scattered. Chose a different gate that they thought had better chances of taking them away from the Cancer or they refused to run anymore or they decided to head back, hoping perhaps that the Cancer had spared a patch of dirt that they could reclaim, rename home. Ash and Palm and baby never saw any of them again.

How many Earths ago was it when they parted ways with the last of that group? Ash tried to remember their names and found out that he couldn't. Tried to remember their faces, but they were blurry. The only thing he could remember, but with a clarity that cut deep, was how his guts twisted at losing them. How existence felt out of line with his soul. He never said anything to Palm, didn't have to. When he looked off into the distance, lost in his thoughts, she slipped a hand onto the small of his back and he touched her arm and that was all the communication that passed between them and the only communication they needed.

But then.

Running through worlds and stumbling through gates with strangers.

Processed (the word sounded like they were meat) together, insulted together. Starved together.

Walking across Earths together, searching for a place where their presence wouldn't offend.

Running together.

He spotted a small group of three that huddled together over a bonfire. Downcast eyes. Tired.

They had been screaming in horror when they ran through the gate away from their world. Did not seem related to each other.

"Cigarette? Cigarette?" he offered. Repeated the word in their language. "Fumo?" Gestured smoking. They in return nodded in appreciation and politely blew their smoke away from baby. Hairless with black bug eyes.

Ash focused for a second and took on their form, eliciting content murmurs from the three.

Baby got startled and slapped him. Pawed at Ash's nose and mouth, making anxious noises. Ash talked to baby until baby was satisfied this was still its father.

They passed food around, the red fruit from the tree attached to a woman's back.

"What's the name?" one of them asked in the group's common language and gestured at baby.

"Nie-méno, no name. Will give name later."

"Later when?"

"When stop running."

They smiled and repeated the words. "When we stop running. Special baby."

"Hoping soon. Hope is free."

_vØ

IT WAS BOUND to happen.

Across an infinite number of universes, there must exist infinite Earths. Infinite possibilities. Infinite dangers.

The iris opened with a sucking sound and the whooshing of air flying past them.

"No atmosphere," Ash whispered.

"Close the gate!" Palm yelled over her shoulder and covered baby's head. Her words, the screams of the people around them, felt echoless.

It only took seconds but it was enough to understand the destruction.

Scorched Earth.

Burning skies, ozone smell.

Colors that did not belong.

A poisonous black sun rained radiation on a lifeless tableau. No. Not lifeless. Only an organic soup, a bacterial mat that heaved and pulsed. But no humanity here. Maybe once. But no more.

This wasn't the Cancer's doing, thought Ash. But this Earth, this universe, was dead to them all the same.

He turned and hugged Palm.

"It's fine. We'll find another gate. We'll move in a different direction. Obviously, this is a dead end. We can't go backwards, but we'll find a way."

"My love…"

"It's fine, it's fine. We'll make it. We'll have to circumvent the dead Earth, go sideways. It can be done."

"My love…"

"It's fine."

"I can't see."

"What?"

"I can't see."

_v4.1

Days passed before Palm said anything.

On the grassy plains of a primitive Earth with its elusive burrow-dwelling humanity she had remained silent and slack-jawed.

When she finally spoke, empty-eyed and cross-legged on the dirt in front of their tent, she stated, "I don't understand."

Ash kissed baby's head and took in the smells. Consecrated sage and heirloom cinnamon. Scent of family. He looked at Palm, shook his head and sighed. "You don't understand, because there is nothing to understand."

"Aren't you going to debate me? Tell me I'm wrong? Aren't you going to tell me that there's intention behind how the universe worked, where I left my sight? How all universes work?"

Ash breathed deeply. "No."

"Why?"

"Because I don't think you're wrong. Because I am starting to think that *we're* all the logic we got."

"Tell me I'm wrong. Tell me this makes sense."

"I'm sorry."

"Give me baby."

Ash put baby into her arms. Watched her whisper into its ear, then he stepped outside.

One of the hairless bugeyed men was standing there. In his outstretched hands, he held a walking stick.

"For Palm. From the rodinah," he said. Community. Ash thought he had misunderstood the word, but that's what it was.

He accepted the stick with a bow as was customary in the hairless man's culture and examined it. Smooth surface. A tangle of roots for a handle that felt remarkably even when he wrapped his hand over it.

"Gratuitos, thank you. It's beautiful."

The hairless man nodded and left.

_v4.2

ASH STEPPED THROUGH the iris. This world smelled of embalmed frankincense and worthless rhinestones.

He motioned at the others.

Palm, who had baby strapped to her back, felt the way with the tip of a smooth walking stick, leading.

Giants from an oxygen-rich Earth.

Hairless bugeyed men.

Twelve-fingered guards from a distant border checkpoint.

Behind them, in the night sky, the stars winked out one by one. Sunk back into nothingness.

Heads low, the group entered and the gate closed behind them.

_v4.3

WHAT'S WRONG WITH that one? The border guard thought-spoke and pointed at Palm, at her silver cataracted eyes that stared into nothing. The guard's words echoed in Ash's head without passing through his ears. Made it easier to communicate/made it feel wrong to communicate.

"She looked straight at a black sun and lost her sight," Ash said out loud, standing at the head of the group. More for their benefit than anything else. Anything he thought, the guard understood.

He did not know where to look on the guard. Not into the eyes, because there were none. Not at the mouth, there was none. Where one would have expected a head between the shoulders, there was nothing. The rest of the body was typical for a human. Two arms with manicured hands, a torso, two legs, two feet in polished black shoes. One of them tap-tap-tapping. Neither Ash nor Palm had shapeshifted into this form, a silent agreement between them to skip it.

Does it carry diseases?

"No."

Anyone carrying diseases?

"No."

That so?

"Yes."

Palm touched Ash's shoulder. "What's going on?"

"Give me a second, I can't concentrate." It took effort for his thoughts to be this crystalline. Not possible to communicate with this human without stilling his mind. And how could his mind be still after so much chaos? The effort it took made him dizzy.

So, no one's carrying diseases. You're a doctor?

"No."

Do you have a doctor among you?

"No."

How many are you?

Ash thought of a thicket of trees. "That many."

You can't get in here.

"Why not?"

You can't.

"Why not?"

Rules.

"What rules?"

Our rules.

"What do those rules say?"

That you can't get in here.

~~You think you're being so clever messing with us~~, Ash tried to suppress the thought.

What was that?

"Nothing."

You can't get in here.

"Where are we supposed to go?"

Don't know. Not here.

"Listen, we got old people here, we got children. We've been running from Earth to Earth."

Why?

"The Cancer."

There is no Cancer.

"We've been running away from the Cancer. Don't tell us it doesn't exist."

There is no Cancer.

"Look at us. Look at us. We don't want to be here." Harder to remain calm now. The headless human's voice distorted in his mind.

What do you want?

"To escape. To settle. Our worlds have been destroyed by this thing. We've all been running away from it."

Ash brought up his memories of lost Earths, lost companions. Focused on the fear. The knots in his stomach every time he understood they had to move again. Brought up the memory of their own world falling apart. Cracked tectonic plates. Mountains moaning into dust. Wondering what waited for them on the other side of that first gate. Palm's terrified face staring at a bloodless sun with the color in her eyes fading.

The guard remained quiet for a long while and Ash had the impression he was cut off from their thoughts.

Your worlds have been destroyed, the guard finally thought. *And you think we'll let you enter and destroy this world too?*

_v4.3

HOW COULD ANYTHING be worse than running?

How could catching your breath be equivalent to being trapped?

Behind them was ruin. A universe turned void. Ahead of them were guards and fences and violence. Not allowed passage, unable to backtrack.

"Suppose we get stuck here." Ash paced back and forth outside their tent, fingers intertwined. His head throbbed from thought-speaking with the headless human, bargaining in vain for hours. He did not look at Palm sitting on the ground with baby in her arms, but at her shimmering shadows on the ground, cast by bonfires across the camp. "Suppose this is the corner we get backed into while the Cancer catches up to us. What then?"

"If it catches up to us, we do as we always do. We run. All of us. Including those guards who keep us here. They can't deny annihilation when it knocks on their door."

"And then what?"

"And then we keep on running."

"Until when?"

"Until we no longer have to."

"And what if that never happens? There are infinite Earths out there. We could be running for eternity."

"Then we run for eternity."

A slight buckle of the knees. A twisting feeling and a realization that Palm was not wrong.

"I can't do that."

"Yes, you can. You just don't want to. That's okay. Neither do I."

"What are we going to do?"

"My love, what *can* we do?"

Ash looked at the headless guards observing them from watchtowers. They should have been observing the skies instead.

"I miss being able to rest."

Palm pushed herself up and shuffled blindly to Ash, embracing him.

_v4.3

ASH GUIDED PALM through the forms they had encountered.

The twelve-fingered humanity.

The humanity with hand-feet.

Even the humanity that never left the seas.

But Palm's gaze remained blank. Sitting on the floor in their tent away from prying eyes, all around her was hair she had shed and horns and claws and beaks and quills and feathers. Sweat coated her skin and she sucked in large mouthfuls of air. She covered her mouth with her arm, lest she wake baby.

"Okay… Let's, let's try the last form. The one I had before

we found the black sun.”

"How about you rest.”

"I'm fine.”

"You're tired.”

"I am tired of being blind and useless. I want to try the last form.”

"How about you try some other one?”

"Because I still remember that form. I got it in my head, I don't need your help.”

"Please. Just save that form for another time.”

Palm stopped and stared in his direction with sightless eyes.

"Why? It has to work. Right? If I *am* able to regain my sight by shapeshifting, it will happen by using the last good form. Right?”

Ash didn't answer.

"Right. So, let's stop wasting time.”

Palm's fingertips vibrated. As her cells settled, as her particles synchronized to the same note, a gasp escaped her mouth.

Ash did not ask Palm if she could see. He shuffled closer to her and embraced her and felt her quivering in impotent anger.

_V4.3

STENCH OF VIOLENCE wafting into the tent. Distant throaty growls. Insults, challenges. Words like bitter almonds.

Palm was up and outside before Ash could shake off the sleep.

"Is it the giants?” she asked.

"Yes.”

The giants. Who surrounded the woman with the tree on her back. Who demanded its fruits. Because they needed more food. Because they were bigger. Explanation and threat.

"Stay away, you might get hurt," Palm said.

"But someone must do something." Baby in Ash's arms was still asleep.

"I know."

The twelve-fingered guards from a distant checkpoint leaped up, put themselves between the woman and the giants.

And the hairless bugeyed men.

And humanity from worlds that no longer existed.

And a blind shapeshifter that shook her walking stick at giants twice her size. Shaming them with her words.

_v4.3

UNEASY DREAMS. DREAMS of being chased. Ash woke with a feeling of unfairness. Was there no respite from being hunted down even in his sleep?

Careful not to wake Palm and baby, he slipped from his sleeping bag and stepped outside the tent. Then another cautious step, and another, until he reached the edge of the camp and sat by the gargling riverbank. No guards here, because they trusted that none of them would be foolish enough to try and cross its thrashing waters. And that suited Ash fine. He longed to be alone just for a little while.

Ash looked up and observed stars that seemed off. Where was Orion and his belt? Where was the Big Dipper? For a moment, panic seized him and he stared hard, counting and begging the stars to remain upon the firmament and not disappear. Begging the moon to continue to shine down on them.

And nothing changed.

And the stars remained, different but soothing.

And panic trailed away and he was left with his thoughts.

His thoughts. The river – incapable of drowning them out. How long before the Cancer found this Earth to the chagrin of those who did not believe in doomsday? How long before they'd have to rip the tent stakes out of the ground again and search, shrieking, for the next gate before being disgorged unto a new Earth? And how would that Earth look?

How long would they be allowed to stay this time?

Because there was no corner in existence that would ever be safe from the Cancer.

He was tired.

Of running. Of hoping. Of adapting. Of adopting. New forms, new languages, new mannerisms. New companions, new companions, new companions.

He was tired.

He was tired.

Didn't realize at first, but he was changing forms. Fingers vibrating so fast they dug into this Earth they were stuck on. Shed his hair, shed his skin. Again. Again.

Horns grew out of his forehead and dropped.

Scales scored his skin and split away, tumbling into the river.

Quills and feathers. Beaks, bills, and bristles, tails, tusks, and talons.

He let it happen, uncaring/unwilling to control it.

Only a recurring thought remained immutable, as constant as humanity across worlds.

We can never stop running. Never stop running.

Ash realized he had passed out when the first rays of the sun woke him. Exhausted from the transformations. The river having lulled him to sleep.

Behind him, people were coming out of their tents, grumbling greetings, coughing, complaining. Smells of morning.

He pushed himself up, an ache deep in his joints. Shuffled back to his tent.

"Ash," a hairless man greeted him.

"Ash," a twelve-fingered guard nodded.

"Ash."

"Ash."

"Ash."

He entered the tent as silently as he could, but Palm was already sitting up feeding baby.

"You couldn't sleep," she stated and Ash could swear she could sense his nodding. "Come closer. Sit."

Ash did as Palm instructed and let her run a hand over him. Touching his hair, his features. Lingering on his lips that wanted to spell out his surrender.

"You feel familiar."

"How so?"

"Hah. I could recognize this face even after a thousand worlds, even after a thousand forms. Hold baby."

Palm took longer to change form. It wasn't perfect. But it was close enough to how Ash remembered her. To how she appeared on the photo.

"It feels off," she said and scrunched her mouth. Her eyes remained blank and her voice cracked. She swallowed, she coughed. "Different."

"Different is fine."

"I'll get it right."

"You got it right."

"I'll get it better."

"Can't get any better."

"Liar."

"I'd never."

"Will you remain this way? For me?"

"I will remain this way."

"And I will remain this way. For you."

_v4.3

ASH WOKE WITH a buzz in his ears, to the smell of burning

108

existence.

In the darkness and blind with sleep, he swept his hand for Palm and touched her sitting form.

"It has a thing for finding us, doesn't it?" she said in the darkness. "You'd think it has a mind of its own. You'd think that we offended it somehow and it won't let go of its grudge."

"You always say it has no will."

"Of course it doesn't. But I hate it regardless."

In the distance, alarms wailed. The camp came to life, voices drifted from the nearby tents. Baby stirred and fussed.

"Where do you suppose the next gate is?" Ash asked.

"The guards might know. They might tell us if they haven't fled already. And if they have, we'll need to find one of the locals and ask."

"If they haven't fled too."

"Obviously."

"Do you need help?"

"No. Yes. Yes, please. Help me dress and give me baby, then guide me outside. I'll try to form a group."

"I'll take care of the rest."

Ash packed their things. Got out and collapsed the tent, removing stakes and folding while looking up—he could have done it in complete darkness with pure muscle memory.

In the sky, the moon was disintegrating, becoming a smudge until it gave way to nothingness. A hole in the night sky that expanded and ate the stars.

Palm was calling out, holding her walking stick in the air, baby strapped to her back. The group gathered around her.

"I bet it's terrifying out there," she said out loud.

No one answered.

"So that's a yes, then. I'm blind and even I can see that nothing ever really changes. We're always on the run, it has become our nature. So, don't be afraid. Pack your things if you haven't already and let's get back on the road. Look after the person next to you; they are the only home you'll ever know."

Ash looked up at the electric smudge that had been the moon and whispered, "Why? What do you want from us?"

In response, stars started blinking out of existence, leaving a blackness behind that hurt to look at. Ash sighed, took Palm's hand, and moved with the others.

As Palm led them towards the camp's abandoned gates, he breathed in deeply. Underneath the smell of the end of this world, he could pick up the scent of their group. Consecrated sage and heirloom cinnamon.

_v5.4

THEY HAD NOT meant to travel this far, this long.

They had not meant to travel.

But here they were.

When was the point that running had turned into a way of life?

Ash tried to remember the exact moment and failed. No one spoke of settling anymore. They argued ways to carry a load so that it wouldn't weigh you down as much. The fastest way to set up a tent and the fastest way to pack it up again. How boiling the gardener's regal red fruit made them sweeter.

"Another Earth."

"Might be the one."

"Hoping is free."

It was the fate of rituals to lose their meaning. Worn-out words that failed to manifest what they sought. At least those words gave comfort. At least that.

The iris opened and they came upon an Earth so unlike the others, so singularly heartbreaking in its beauty, that for long moments they forgot that they were running. Forgot that they were capable of running. Forgot that they could do anything other than admire the cosmic casting of the dice that led to the sights greeting them past the gates.

"There are no guards," Ash said. "No processing station. Nothing."

"What do you see?" Palm asked.

"I see mountains. Alpine lakes glistening between their peaks. Thick forests; looks like cedars. Could it be cedars? And there's a slight salty breeze coming from the South."

"I can feel the breeze."

"And it smells wonderful here. Timeless cloves. Slumbering sands."

Ash closed his eyes and thought of the Cancer finding this world and his chest hurt. He pushed the thought out of his mind.

The group set up camp in a clearing at the foot of the mountains. Ash and the hairless bug-eyed men surveyed the area but couldn't find humanity. Returned perplexed as the sun dipped below the horizon.

"Maybe in a few thousand years," he said to his companions. "Maybe I was wrong about the universe," he said to Palm. "Maybe it doesn't need us."

Palm was preparing the camp fire with others. Skewered root vegetables lay on the grass ready to be roasted.

"Come and sit with me," Palm said and motioned in the rough direction of a log. Ash helped her sit. "Where is she?"

Baby was running around the firepit, picking up twigs, throwing them in.

"Being helpful," Ash replied.

"We'll need to name her. She's gone long enough being no-one."

"We don't have a name still."

Palm went quiet and Ash could tell she was taking in the sounds surrounding them. Sounds of a camp gathering wood, preparing food. Languages converging.

Off in the distance, twelve-fingered guards from a border that no longer existed argued with giants on the best way to fell a tree.

The rattling of quills on someone's head as they gathered mushrooms.

The clicking of someone's beak as they instructed on how to set up a tent.

Once in a while, someone would look up from their work towards the mountains, white against the firmament, and their sighs of wonder made it to Ash and Palm's ears.

A small group had gathered around a fire and told stories of worlds gone by—in languages that increasingly sounded as one. The woman with a tree strapped to her back weaved between them and handed them red fruit, receiving gratitude.

"I know of a tree that exists across all worlds, all Earths," Palm said. "Seems like a fitting name."

"A fitting name," Ash said.

About The Author

EA Mylonas is a photographer, writer and author of the speculative fiction novel *The Hush*.

Originally from Athens, Greece, he has spent the last couple of decades travelling and working through the world. In that time, he's tended to wounded loggerhead turtles, baked bread for a Michelin-star restaurant and written dialogues for video games.

An environmental scientist by training, he is an advocate for the climate cause, sustainable living and anti-corporatism, which inspire his unique brand of literary sci-fi. He spends his free time trail-running, hiking and rock climbing.

Villainous

Hugo Jackson

Sirens wailed in the supercity of New Menagerie. Flashing blue lights dazzled along the highway, reflecting off the passing skyscrapers at pelting speeds.

The sleek black-and-bronze frame of the motorbike almost blended into the night of faded orange fluorescent streetlights and dark concrete, save for its silken electrical whine and trail of light burning its way through traffic. The helmeted rider's narrow cape fluttered behind them just above their tail, enrobed in its sleek protective armour. They glanced in their wing mirror, regarding the pursuing officers as if they were barely there.

The rider was watching for something different.

They listened to the police chatter coming through their earpiece.

"—in pursuit of unknown villain on highway NM-53, potential super; target has hit several medical sites this evening. Consider armed or powered. No positive response from Darkwolf…"

The rider looked ahead.

Something crossing the sky caught their line of sight. Just visible past the streetlamps' haze, a bolt of silver against the stars.

There you are.

EARLIER THAT DAY

A TALL, MUSCULAR wolf with fur that glistened with a sheen of silver crossed the hall of his house. Around his head was a thick-strapped eyepatch of black leather bordered with silver and purple. Over his shoulder was a gym towel that barely covered his bulky limb, as his paw grasped onto it and showed off the rope-like muscles of his arm, covered in purple markings like blades in silhouette. His tank top left little of his muscles to the imagination, but being in his own home, there weren't any voyeurs or paparazzi to worry about.

He glanced into the bedroom as he passed, seeing the still-slumbering form of his vulpine partner on the wide bed. The sound of a water wall at one end rippled lightly through the quiet space. It was a gentle scene, soft, but he knew within the room was something more quieting than sleep.

His fox hadn't been the same since the incident. Over the months he'd grown morose, less talkative, slept far far more than he used to, and obviously, they could no longer go on their hero sprees together like they used to.

Orion couldn't blame him. The fox had almost died.

He worried, in some way, that he actually had.

The papers had been merciless in their appetite for gossip.

"DUSKFOX OUT OF ACTION? DASHING DUO DOWN TO SOLO SAVIOUR!"

"From Hero to Hermit: The Painful Isolation of Duskfox."

"A New Flame? Darkwolf Sees Mission Completed With Astra, Psychic Lynx!"

Whoever said "sticks and stones may break my bones but words shall never hurt me" had never been subjected to eighteen months of newspaper speculation and unwarranted, invasive 'exposés' of their private life, formed on nothing but malicious wish fulfilment by media scroungers filling their pockets with the revenue of speculation, outrage and advertising.

It would have made Darkwolf quit, or move, had he the choice. But someone with powers like his had to keep his duty to the city. To protect. That's what heroes were: lawful. Against the lawless. Throwing himself into duties of protection was what kept him focused, to provide for his recovering partner and hope they could someday find some peace and comfort together.

He didn't know when that day would be. Nor what he could do to reach him. But he'd try, always.

A noise pinged on his wrist watch. A new tip had come in that he had to follow up on, after a recent smash-and-grab on a pharmaceutical truck carrying an allegedly invaluable cargo of drugs.

He entered the dimly-lit bedroom and sat on the bed, gently reaching his paw over to rouse the resting fox.

"Cymbel? You alright?"

The fox rolled over and grunted, showing off the mechanics that had been installed in his chest to save him from death.

"M'okay," he mumbled back, eyes half-lidded, and still blinking away sleep.

The wolf leant down and kissed the diamond marking between the fox's eyes. "I have to leave. I just... wanted to see you before I did."

The fox sighed gently, letting his head fall to the side. "I slept that long again?"

Orion stroked his paw sympathetically at Cymbel's shoulder. "It's... we'll work something out."

Cymbel planted his head a little more firmly into the pillow, turning somewhat roughly. "We've been saying that for months." There was a pause, and he let out a rough, sharp breath. "Sorry. I'm just... tired. Tired of being tired."

"I know, love. I'll…" The wolf didn't really have any words. He'd come away from the explosive altercation with The Surgeon missing only his eye, while Cymbel had taken the full force of the supervillain's hit in the chest. If Darkwolf hadn't immediately shrouded the fox in his starlight magic and torn through the sky to the hospital, Cymbel would have died in the cold of the underground lair.

I'll do what I can. I'll save you. I'll find something that brings you back to me. I'll take care of it all.

"I'll see you when I get back, okay? Rest well for me."

Cymbel looked coldly into the waterwall.

"What other choice is there?"

The wolf looked down as he stood, letting his paw slip from his fox, and padded out of the bedroom.

PRESENT TIME

THE RIDER ACCELERATED, leaning into their handlebars. The bike's twin engines roared, and they began to peel away from the chase.

The bolt of silver banked in the sky, narrowed, remained still for just a moment, and then thundered towards them at unearthly speed. They swerved the bike just in time to miss the explosion in the concrete that burst in front of them. The bike fishtailed and almost toppled, but they managed to right themself and begin another accelerating run.

From the crater though, another flash of movement. A tall, bulky wolf of silver fur and jagged purple markings darted from the cloud of debris and slammed into their vehicle, sending it spinning into the concrete barrier. The rider leapt from it, *barely*, and rolled to a low, ready stance in the street. A baton whipped from their thigh, sparking with red flecks of electricity.

The wolf turned to them, raising his bold, thick muzzle. His left eye was covered in a dark eyepatch emblazoned with a sigil of a silver wolf's head, with a trail of lightning behind it. His super suit was a sleeveless, armoured bodysuit of purple with a deep silver V travelling down his chest to his beltline, and fingerless gloves with long cuffs. A cape similar to the rider's, but wider, gathered around his neck and swept over his shoulders.

"Ride's over," he growled.

The villain said nothing as Darkwolf regarded them, gaze unable to pierce the reflective tint of their angular helmet. He could glean no indication of species, though the length of the tail was impossible to hide even in its protective compression sheath. Canine – small, or perhaps feline or mustelid. They were a relatively slight figure, shorter than him (though considering his size, that was true for most creatures he encountered), and holding what looked like a power disruptor baton in their right paw.

"Your toy won't stop me," he warned, stepping forwards.

The rider remained in their stance, weapon flickering with crimson fulminations.

"Have it your way."

Darkwolf blitzed forwards, leaving a trail of silver along the torn ground. The slender figure darted aside and swept out the weapon, striking Darkwolf on the leg. Orion felt his energy drain instantly from that limb; he collapsed, carving a rut in the ground as he skidded to a stop, before wrenching himself back up to launch a bolt of starlight from his palm.

The assailant parried it with the red lightning; the shot of silver-gold streaked off into a nearby building, splintering concrete and glass into the street below.

Darkwolf glared, teeth beginning to dance with sparks.

THAT AFTERNOON

THE WOLF LEANT on his knee as he dangled a leg from the edge of the building he was sat on, watching the city below.

Dozens, hundreds of cars moving along elevated roadways, utility vehicles chuntering away on the ground level between buildings and streets that barely ever saw real daylight.

It was far from a perfect city, but he would protect it in every way he could. For one thing, it was where his home was. The place Cymbel was.

Though there was a certain emptiness to it. He could both understand, and not, how the fox had become so sullen and withdrawn. Orion could only assume it was down to the fatigue of the mechanical organs and muscles he'd had implanted, a malaise perhaps of being unable to do what had been one of his most defining activities, one that he'd formerly talked about so proudly.

Orion was the one with the greatest powers, the silver-born magic related to starlight and the night sky, but Cymbel had been the one to really inspire him to find a use for it and give himself greater purpose. The fox's powers were more akin to using shadows to move through and perceive the space around him, with incredible reflexes and resilience; as such he'd been able to pursue and keep up with Darkwolf since they first started interacting. To be carrying on without him felt somewhat empty, beyond the thrill of a chase or vengeful satisfaction of a villain caught.

Darkwolf had to admit that immediately following Cymbel's injury, he had been enthralled by violent retribution. When not at his partner's bedside, the vehemence had been translated into greater direct force against villainy. It took him away from Cymbel, though it was necessary. For himself. A problem he could punch or burn away, unlike his love's affliction.

Cymbel's waking thoughts had not been of much comfort, and for a time had darkened the wolf's demeanour further. There was no shortage of despondency. They'd argued about how deadly Orion needed to be, and the wolf began to observe a change in the way Cymbel saw those considered 'hindrances' to the city. Their motivations, mainly. The sense of sympathy was somewhat alien to the wolf, though the aftermath of his fights had begun to haunt him as he witnessed shades of the state Cymbel was left in. Many of the villains he came across even *before* battle had been hurt to the point of disfigurement, tortured, abandoned, forced to make their own way. Some of them as a result of prior heroic encounters, whether accidental or deliberate.

And there was the collateral. Orion was careful in his technique, but accidents were inevitable. Powers weren't a guarantee of increased stamina or health regeneration, and of course, civilians or powered individuals not signed up to any municipal hero groups didn't get awarded New Menagerie City Government health insurance. From what Darkwolf was told, any misfortunes under the licensed hero activity were processed 'adequately'. Anyone considered outside their responsibility had to fend for themselves – villains and civilians.

He and Cymbel had begun to disagree on that lately, too. Orion didn't understand why.

Cymbel had said something that circled his head every time he flew to a crime scene. *"If the only difference between hero and villain is the law, who are you really protecting?"*

He'd thought at the time it was a more rhetorical question born out of bitterness from the muted success of the prosthetics. Survival, but not recovery. The Circle of Valour, considered the highest echelon of heroic covenant, had expressed sympathy at the city's 'loss' of Duskfox, and had tried to set up replacements. A strange and rather cold consideration, because the fox wasn't 'lost', he was still there, even though his powers had yet to fully return. Orion had turned every prospective candidate down, to the point that it created tension with the Circle. Advocating for giving his own partner time was, apparently, divisive. Avoiding press opportunities to care for his fox had also drawn some derision, though many heroes were keen to soak up space at the podium.

Someone had left gifts, however, outside their home. Mobility aids. Prosthetic easements and adjustment monitors. Some suspicious tech that Darkwolf had assumed was a bomb at first, but Cymbel had saved. All anonymous. He could only speculate it was a Circle member who wanted to provide aid in the only way they were permitted.

But this alternative idea, that someone as far away from the Circle as anyone could possibly be, had left it instead – had pervaded Orion regardless of its unlikeliness. Orion had expected taunts. Most villainous adversaries had been strangely respectful of Cymbel when he was mentioned, and criticism was thrown more at Darkwolf's allegiance to an oppressive system than the fox. A sense of honour, maybe, towards a more innocent fallen nemesis than if it had been the wolf himself. But Orion wondered if there was something more sinister among those who regarded him favourably. A creeping sensation that they recognised how Cymbel's peers did not look kindly upon his injuries, the peers who had all but considered him retired as soon as they saw him in the hospital bed (the few who visited outside their junkets and PR-curated photo opportunities, anyway).

He worried sometimes that a villain might see more in Cymbel than a hero could. An understanding that even he couldn't yet reach.

It was pushing him into considerations he hadn't ventured through before. That the villains were who they were out of circumstance and not ontological malice. With how much he had seen directly, the danger they had wrought, the times he and Cymbel had put their lives on the line to stop them, when the conversation inevitably turned on him it inflamed his temper, and left the two in echoing silence through their house. He had a duty to protect the stability of the city, and keep the citizenry safe, no matter the reasons for the villains' choices.

And Cymbel, for all his doubts, was still a hero.

Nothing would change that.

He rolled his wrist over to check the holographic display on his watch. No hits from the drug thief yet. The New Menagerie PD had suggested they were looking to sell the stolen chemicals on the black market or form some kind of super serum that might take down prominent heroes. The sensationalism was rather rampant, especially with the city's star duo at the moment only working at half capacity.

He scratched his muzzle and sighed while he waited for the call to come in, as above, the sun began to curve towards the horizon.

PRESENT TIME

THE WOLF'S TEETH brimmed with plasma-like trails as his jaw opened; a shining burst of silver-white exploded from him and shrieked through the air towards the rider. They dove away but the searing white flooded their vision and singed their cape. They stumbled slightly, and that was Darkwolf's chance. He followed his burst with a lopsided, limping lunge, claws out, ready to catch the villain between them. He swiped; the villain retaliated with a swing of their baton and stole the energy from the wolf's arm. His limb flinched and jerked; Darkwolf's other claw swung in and managed to knock the stun device away. As the rider dived for it, the starry lupine released another blast from his maw towards it. The baton was completely vaporised, along with a good portion of the concrete it had fallen to.

The rider shirked back, deftly swirling away, once more coming to stare down the wolf.

Darkwolf flexed his limp paw to bring some feeling back to it and to pump the energy through it again. Little drips of starlight oozed from his clawtips, unable to be adequately contained or metered out.

"Take your helmet off, coward."

The rider remained poised, unmoving aside from their tail, which flexed slowly behind them.

Darkwolf's eye narrowed, a scornful look curling his maw. "Pathetic. Just an errant thief out to score blood money."

A bitter synthetic chuckle met his ears, and nothing more.

With a bark of anger the wolf charged forwards again, light streaming from his claws, throwing them forwards to release a helixing beam towards the rider. They fell backwards beneath it and rolled back to their bike. With a swift kick the paniers opened, revealing the sacks of stolen drugs which they swept over their shoulders. The rider stood by their broken vehicle, and performed a brief, somewhat mocking salute.

Darkwolf charged, arm thrusting forwards with star-tipped claws. The canine's paw plunged into the body of the bike; light shimmered and erupted from its seams and a split second later the vehicle exploded in a burst of molten metal, fire, and tiny stars.

The rider had ducked away, albeit barely, and glared at him over the white-hot wreckage. The synthetic voice buzzed stridently in the wolf's ears.

"Out of time, Darkwolf. Soon we shall know the true measure of you."

Before he could even whirl round, a strange, rippling distortion overtook the rider, and when his eye adjusted, they were gone.

For a moment he stood in the centre of his carnage, with the police cars still waiting nearby. A small scrap of the rider's cape, blasted by his starfire, fluttered around the burning crater. He took it in his claw and turned it over. It smelt of nothing but char and ozone, but he might have a way of tracking it. The flashing of the cop's lights was drawing his increasing ire, and now they were beginning to storm out and yelling commands or acting as his 'backup'. A low growl rattled in his throat. Eager to avoid their abrasive overbearance, after a brief test of his drained limbs he took to the sky in a flash of light, and a low, rumbling *boom*.

LATER

HE PATROLLED THE sky for over an hour, ignoring other calls that came in over his device. That rider had dug their fangs into him, left him marked with ravening intrigue.

He had to know who they were.

He flipped up his watch, which displayed a holographic image of Cymbel's face, still dressed in his hero outfit of a hooded cape and face mask.

Will be late tonight. Sorry, love, he typed with a claw on the shimmering incorporeal keypad that materialised in front of him. Once the message was sent, he continued his flying scan of the city. New Menagerie was sprawling. It was almost impossible to see anything except the expanse of tangled concrete and jutting glass buildings. 'Industrial expansion', they called it, though they didn't seem to understand it robbed him of a stronger connection to the empyrean.

He'd get nowhere tonight like this. He had enough power left for a divining, and then he'd be left with physical strength alone. Floating above a crossroads, he dipped into the pocket of his suit and pulled out the scrap of cape. It took a lot of energy, but he was running out of options if he wanted to get back to Cymbel tonight.

He drew all ten of his claws together, with the cape shred at their centre. They all bloomed with gentle light. He withdrew them, spreading and spiralling his hands, forming a web that held the small piece of charred fabric at its centre. Brow furrowing under the effort of coalescing his reserves of energy, he let out a long, controlled breath, as he turned in place. The shred flicked as he moved, but when he faced the older part of town under a nest of highways, it tugged more forcefully, trying to escape the web.

That was his bearing.

He took flight, following its movements. It guided him between skyscrapers, across the city and down, sweeping under bridges and highways to bring him to the lowest street level. He eased his speed, allowing him to control his astral levitation as he swept through the brick and concrete buildings. Glass panes were coated with a thick layer of indistinct brown grime, a mix of fumes from trains and cars, and detrital sediment that could be brought no lower than here.

The shred pulled towards a building that looked like an old hotel, before his ability to sustain the star-guided tracking dissipated, and his paws touched down on the aged, torn asphalt. The hotel's windows were boarded up, but there were lights flickering from between the panels, and a gentle rotation of people coming in and out of it.

A message pinged on his watch.

Cymbel.

See you soon, love.

A brief, half-smile graced his muzzle before the message faded out and he returned his focus to the criminal foretold within the old, grimy hotel. Was it a brothel now? A drug house?

He alighted the ground, and strode towards it.

The doors barely resisted his forceful push: they sailed open and buckled at their rusting hinges, silhouetting the wolf against the dying street lamps. Some creatures waiting in line at the reception counter began running for other rooms, and the rest just watched in awestruck fear as Darkwolf made his prowling scan of the room. Heavy paws cracked the aging tiles, muscular shoulders flexed with tension and gleaming claws shone in the dim foyer. A resonant growl rolled through his fangs, pulsing with his steady, strong breaths.

The old checkerboard tile was chipped, dirty, none of their colours matching what they once were. The lobby opened up to mezzanines of the four floors above. At the ceiling's apex was a large domed skylight that would once have let in the light, not that there was any left to grace it under the highway and decades of gaseous sediment. On the counter behind the desk were the bags the rider had pulled from their bike, now empty. Strewn around the floor were boxes that had the logos of several pharmaceutical companies emblazoned on them, the bounty already torn open.

Whatever they were making, it was quite a cocktail.

The citizens were unimportant for now. Ignorant until proven otherwise. He looked around, casting his eye over them all, hunting for the rider.

"Show yourself!" he barked. His voice rattled loose panels.

The trapped bystanders flinched and looked at each other fearfully. He stepped forwards. "I said—"

"I heard you," came the synthetic voice once more. The rider emerged from behind the reception area, holding a small canister in their gloved paw. "Wasn't expecting you to find me so soon, I have to admit. I had hoped you'd have worn yourself out by now."

They beckoned one of the citizens forward, a rather meek-looking skunk who definitely did not want to be there anymore, and handed the canister to them.

"You should probably leave. All of you. I'll do my best to keep this quiet," they said, casting their head back round to the intruding hero.

As the skunk took the little jar, Darkwolf approached, about to place a paw on the skunk to halt him and see what the canister contained. The skunk yelped and cowered, curling around the can. Just as the wolf reached him, the rider thrust their arm to Darkwolf's chest in a halting motion, allowing the skunk to retreat.

"You know better than to assault civilians, Darkwolf."

The hero growled, clasping the villain's wrist in his paw. They didn't resist. "What are you giving them?"

The rider looked around briefly, slowly, almost with a languid air of tiredness, then angled their helmet back at him. "Hope."

"Hope?" he growled. "With crime? With drugs?"

To his surprise, the rider sighed. Their body seemed to be moving with their breaths – tiredness, perhaps? "The right ones, yes. You'd be surprised how effective they are in tipping the balance."

Darkwolf had had enough. With a growling roar he swept his arm back into the rider's chest, bowling them over the reception desk and onto the floor behind it.

The wolf gnarled again and leapt down, bringing his fist to the floor (although it was intended to be the rider's helmet) in a blow strong enough to make the desk shift from its anchors and shatter tiles. The rider was pinned beneath the wolf now, head tilted to one side, barely an inch from the impact crater. Darkwolf could hear the rider's breath push against the synthesiser, producing buzzing rasps of effort and danger. Was this all they had? Though his own reserves were also equally depleted by the divination and the hunt.

Regardless, he had his physical strength, and pressed on.

"What are you trying to do? Make supersoldiers? Addicts? Mind control?"

The rider laughed, a bitter and slightly offended noise, with a hoarseness to their voice. "You're in the wrong part of your head, Darkwolf. None of those would bring about what I want. They would only make things worse."

The wolf scowled, leaning in. "Your ambitions end here." He hooked a claw under the helmet. "Now we get to see who you are."

"You might not like…"

Before the rider could finish, Darkwolf twisted the helmet free. The fox within looked back up at him, with eyes of blazing, familiar green.

"C… Cymbel?"

"Was it really that hard?" his fox replied, exhausted voice somehow a mix of disappointment and affection. "I thought you'd know me the moment I disappeared."

They were frozen together, a tableau of shock and stalled

combat. Orion's threats melted away, thawing out a thousand questions from underneath them. His jaw tightened, his face tensed into a grimacing, pained sneer. The shadowy ripple that enveloped the rider – the connection was made instantly now, and he cursed himself for being so focused on winning the fight that he lost the details. He closed his eye, trying to shake away what was becoming a rather fast headache. "You… you were home. You… had been…"

Cymbel reached a paw up to Orion's cheek. "I've been doing this for weeks, love," he breathed, rather laboured. "Every night, while you were gone, I'd train. And upgrade. Just enough, bit by bit, to get myself moving again. Until I could start making heists."

"Did you… who gave you the upgrades?"

The fox shook his head, and groaned with a rather lopsided smile. "They don't give these out legally, pet. You can thank Brassfire."

The wolf swept the paw at his face away, with a renewed expression of vengeance. "The dragon sharpshot? He's a *villain*! Have you any idea how that compromises our safety? Our position?" His breath was hot and his tone as sharp as the fangs that framed it. "And *yourself*?! You could have died, Cymbel!"

The fox looked away, seemingly unconcerned about that particular consequence. "I've been looking over that precipice for a long time, Orion," he said quietly. He looked back up to him, briefly, a little shamefully, perhaps, before his eyes tracked back down again, and once more raised his paw rather weakly to Orion's chest. "I'm not trying to hurt you, I promise."

The wolf's snarl remained, body tense. He recoiled slightly at his fox's touch, but let it stay. His claw was raised as if to tear something to shreds, but he was unable to lower it even an inch towards his beloved. He let a chill ripple through his fur as he stared back into those wonderful, forlorn eyes, and spat a bitter sigh.

"Talk, Cymbel. Is this all for you? Is someone blackmailing

you, controlling you?"

The fox closed his eyes, head hitting the floor in rather tired exasperation. "No, no no, pet." He opened his eyes and looked back into Orion's. "I'm not a bloody automaton. I chose this. Just me." He kept his gaze fixed on his dark hero. "Do you even know what those meds were? Did nobody tell you?"

The wolf's brow furrowed. "Meds?"

Cymbel smiled sardonically. "I know that doesn't have the same ring as 'drugs', but they are what they are." He flicked his muzzle towards the back. "Go and check. I can't run from you anymore."

His breathing haggard, Orion wrenched himself up and stormed into the back, where the boxes of drugs, alongside several that looked to have been from previous raids, were lined out on the back office counter. With them were sanitised bottles, needles, and other medical paraphernalia. Closer inspection brought an end to one avenue of speculation for the hero. Pain meds. Antibiotics. Heart medication. Anti-cancer treatments. Antivirals.

He'd set up a pharmacy. The companies had made what he'd taken sound illicit, dangerous. Compromising.

He turned; as he did he saw his fox leaning against the reception desk, with a weak smile. His breathing was laboured. Orion wasn't sure how to react, where to start.

"You could have told me," was all he could manage.

The fox tilted his head back with a sigh. "That would have been the 'honourable' thing, wouldn't it?" He looked back down, softly, and rather forlorn. "Been a while since I felt I fit that word."

A cold, slight breath of amusement rushed from Orion's nose. "You were always more honourable than I was." He looked at Cymbel briefly, then away again. "So… what changed? Why do all this? Why not a charity, a drive, or something?"

"Because it's never enough!" Cymbel's voice, empowered by his bitterness, rang in the empty, dusty foyer. The words hung in the air before he had to hold the desk for balance once more, and coughed into his paw. "You… you don't know what it's like, to have your body torn apart. To feel hollow. And then worse," he spat, "to be forgotten, *deliberately*, by all of the people who always moralised about how 'good' they were."

Orion could only respond with guilty silence.

"Do you know that tiredness hurts?" Cymbel continued. "It burns. Eats a hole in your chest and mind that all of your words and fears fall into. Your life shrinks. But outside it is a fiery darkness of all of the things that haunt you – the plans you lost, the people who left, the futures pulled away. I had to do something, Orion. I don't want to watch my body turn to dust with me inside it."

"But *villainy?*" The wolf opened his arms. "You'd do this instead of fighting for heroes again?"

Cymbel jabbed a claw his way. "What do your heroes *do*, Orion? Where do you see them helping people like this? Like me? They throw out grand gestures at community parks and save a skyscraper but where do you see *any* of them, a *single* one, looking out for these people? People who don't need saving only once, but every day?"

He held a paw to his chest. "It's broken, Orion. Everything is broken. And this – taking from the corporations who dangle people's own lives in front of their faces for money – is the way to set things right."

He stood taller, with a stab of pain in his chest that made him wince. "We've been defending the wrong people."

Orion looked between his partner, the meds, the cowering folk in the shadows of the foyer. "The… it's a crime—"

"Get out of your head, Orion!" Cymbel's voice ripped from his throat. "Pain is a crime! And these people are twisting the knife in all of our backs." He pointed at the wolf's eye. "You lost that eye the day I lost my heart to The Surgeon. You were given help because of who you were, and I was too. In service of the city. If nobody knew your name, you'd have your whole life from that point on defined by the money you were never able to pay back. An injury made insult. *That's* the crime."

The wolf shook his head. "You can't do this."

"No, we *haven't* done this." He flexed his shoulders back, still weakened, standing shorter than the imposing, muscular wolf, but providing a presence to match. "But we should. And I will keep doing it, unless you stop me."

Orion's fists clenched. He shook his head. "I… can't do that, Cymbel. But I can't let you continue."

"Then what?" The fox threw out his arms. "I'll stay at home for the rest of my life? Watching you save business after business while everyone talks over me about how sad it is that I don't exist anymore? Knowing our fights have done so much worse to those who have no powers to recover with, no city-mandated care to float them? I won't go back to it, Orion."

The wolf's chest was beginning to rise faster, in deeper, sharper breaths.

"Do you… do you think you were the only one hurt when you were on the edge of death?"

Cymbel stayed firm, but his eyes began to glisten, and only misted further as the wolf began to speak.

"Did you know how terrified I was of losing you? How terrified I still am that I could come home any day and find you gone, your body failed, or taken from me by those who want to hurt us?" He marched forwards and slammed his paw on the counter, leaning over Cymbel. "Do you think it was easy for me watching you die over and over again on the operating table while they hammered those parts into you, wondering if I'd ever get to see you again? That I imagine every night might be the final time I get to tell you how much I love you?"

Aside from Orion's breaths and words, the room was deathly silent.

"I have done everything to keep you safe. Keep us going, so you could come back. I have not stopped thinking about how close you were to leaving, and I… it…" His claws rattled on the wood as he tried to resist the tremble in his arm. "It is the thing that scares me most in this world."

Gently, Cymbel raised a paw to the hero's chest again. For a moment they touched, then the wolf turned his head and pulled away, running his hands over his muzzle and ears. The fox followed for a step.

"I… never wanted any of this to happen. What eats me every day is I can't tell if this was a good thing or not." His voice cracked a little. "I could have lived in ignorance, never knowing, but healthy. But now I… everything hurts. Some days I can barely stand." He laughed, bitterly. "It took me a week to rest up for tonight even with the mechanic boosts, and I'll be out for days afterwards. Being awake can be torture, trapped in a body that won't listen to how much I scream for it to move. But now I know where the cracks in the world are that we fall through, and it's… it's terrifying, Orion," he whispered.

The wolf turned back, face low, morose. "Did you think I wouldn't be there for you, at every step of the way?"

Cymbel moved to the wolf's side, and took his paw. "I knew you would. But every time you said 'it's okay, I'm here' – while *yes*, that means everything – the cry in my mind was that *I* still need to have a life and purpose. You told me *you'll* fix it, *you'll* make things right, but where am I in that?" he wavered, voice cracking further. "Do I even get to tell you how it feels, what I actually need from you, and myself? I'm here, broken but not shattered, still here!" He brought Orion's paw to his own chest, gripping it tightly. "I don't want to exist as a proxy for your guilt, or just be a vessel of love that does nothing but sit and be grateful for your dedication! Hell, maybe before I lost my heart the idea of aimless luxury was a great one: crime's solved, you can retire now!"

He gripped his love's paw tighter. "But now… I can't escape this. I can never unfeel what it's like to be forgotten. Left behind. And I'm *lucky* – I was given a chance to live again but these people won't! They have *this* chance at life and that's *it*! As heroes we paraded around what we did for the city as if that mattered to anyone except some generic mass of able-bodied nine-to-five people we never met, and bigwigs who'd throw us expensive thank you parties for saving their stock prices. And now you're expected to save the companies who hold millions like this hostage for money? Means-testing their own damn *lives*? It's barbaric, Orion!"

He gently nudged his snout under the wolf's, trying to bring their eyelines together once more. He succeeded, barely, but once he had the wolf in his gaze they were unable to part once again. "This isn't a betrayal. It's *honesty*. It's what we should always have been."

He paused, facing his partner nose-to-nose, eyes glistening in the light of the broken hotel. Their breaths mingled, their heartbeats pulsed through each other's paws.

Orion closed his eye. Gently, he leant in, and took Cymbel into his arms. They held each other for a long time in silence, pressing their chests together, before the fox gently slipped back, and smiled up at his partner.

"So, *hero*, what will you do with me?"

TWO WEEKS LATER

[A STREAMING VIDEO plays on a computer screen. Its title is 'DarkWolf DEFECTS? Where Is The Media?' A raccoon against a green screen has a still image of a burning Darkwolf logo behind him.]

Can you believe it, hero fans? New Menagerie and all of us inside it were left stunned today when Darkwolf was revealed to be the source behind the massive thefts from pharmaceutical companies in recent weeks. After skipping a press summit earlier this morning, where Darkwolf was supposed to be announcing a new crimefighting initiative aimed at tackling drug thieves, instead he released his own video openly refusing to protect the companies and OPENLY THREATENING THEM INSTEAD! Here's the clip:

"When I swore to protect this city, for a time I forgot what that meant. I put my sense of achievement into congratulatory statements and parties where city officials lobbied alongside corporations for my protection. But they are not who make this city, nor the world, what it is. The people of New Menagerie have been torn apart, trampled, held at knifepoint, had their heritages destroyed for the profit of developers and billionaires.

"It took me far too long to see that a 'hero' in the eyes of the rich is one who protects profits over people.

"I am no longer that protector. Until you align with the safety of those people whose heads you step on every day to reach your glass castles, I will be their vengeance.

"If that makes me your enemy, so be it. Better an honourable villain than a toxic hero."

*Did you catch that? INSANE! And **then**, Darkwolf shattered the atrium of the X-Med Plaza, a building that was protested for being erected in the city's former green belt. And here's the kicker: Duskfox is all-in on this too! And, and! Both of them have **also** warned that land developers and gun manufacturers will be next!*

*The media's said **nothing** about this! Can you believe it? Trying to pretend this threat to our jobs and livelihoods just doesn't exist! But is it for the best — can we even survive DarkWolf's wrath if we make him angry? What's going to happen to all our businesses? Can anyone even own anything anymore? Can one of the most powerful entities to ever inhabit New Menagerie, even be stopped? Keep your windows closed and your curtains drawn, 'cause a **bad** storm's coming…*

About The Author

Hugo is a British-born author living in North Carolina. They began life as a starry-eyed creature with a fascination for fantastical adventures, heroes, and animals, and invested as much time in their own imagination as they did on animations, video games, and music.

They began writing their first novel, *Legacy*, in 2006, which was to become the first in a series of four called *The Resonance Tetralogy*. It was released 2010, and in 2013 it was republished with great pride under Inspired Quill's banner. This was followed in 2016 by *Fracture*. Since then the series has been completed with the release of *Ruin's Dawn* and, most recently, *Edge of Ascension*.

In 2012 Hugo moved to the United States to live with their wife Madison, who is a native to North Carolina, where they both enjoy as much barbecue and biscuits as health will reasonably allow, and together dote over a lovely corgi-cross named Tohru.

In their spare time, Hugo is heavily involved with the furry fandom, standing as an advocate for LGBT+ rights, mental health awareness, inclusion, and artist/author visibility and fair treatment.

Not Her

Alex Westmore

River Valley, California

BULLETS PINGED ALL around Delta Stevens as she knelt behind a utility meter and considered her limited options. Her partner, Miles Brookman, had ordered her to stay in the safety of the patrol car, but when the shooter blew out the back window, she chose a different route and bailed out to scurry over to the rectangular army green meter that now acted as a shield.

This wasn't at all what being in the Police Academy had been like. They'd gone over domestic violence, gang issues, even hostage situations, but they'd never covered this what-if scenario of a heavily armed shooter taking pot shots at them from inside a building.

She wasn't the least bit surprised, of course. In the state of California, it took nine months to become a licensed hairdresser. It only took three and a half to pass her Police Officers Standard Test.

Think about that for a moment.

Yeah. There's all sorts of wrong with that, and Delta understood, out of the gate, that the Keystone Cops were alive and well in every police department. The lack of training was why cops made so many mistakes.

She used to lie in bed at night haunted by that fact. It was no wonder so many cops screwed up so often. You can't give a twenty-three-year-old boy a gun and all of the power of God and expect him to make wise decisions after less than four months of training.

Nine times out of ten, they didn't. Make wise decisions, that is.

Still, The Academy had been fun for the nearly six-foot tall Delta Stevens, nicknamed Storm; a moniker she received from the guys in her academy for the way she stormed into the simulations, unafraid, unbothered by the fact that so many rookies failed their first time out.

Not her.

She knew it was all a game. One big game. The superior officers, who didn't really want to be teaching at The Academy, and the rookies, who would do just about anything for a morsel of praise, were unequal opponents because of the power dynamic. The officers strutted around like the cocks of the walk, an air of stale superiority wafting around them. They were not the cream of the crop, to be sure. No, they had been relieved of regular duty for one reason or another, so there were a few shoulder chips on display.

They enjoyed pushing the cadets around, but still managed to dole out their praise to people who, apparently, needed it.

Not her.

No. Delta Stevens needed no one else to tell her she was good. Police work came naturally to her, as if she had been born wearing a badge.

Maybe she had been.

She remembered so clearly the first time she saw a female officer stand up to a much taller man who tried to push by her to continue beating his wife.

Two seconds later, the man was in a wrist lock with his face driven into the pavement, the cop whispering something in his ear as she ground his face into the dirty street.

Ten-year-old Delta had just stood there in awe of the

much smaller woman now in complete control of the situation and the very aggressive perpetrator.

When the cop realized Delta was watching, she winked at her. "Never let a man hurt you," she said, yanking him to his feet. "Without making him pay."

Something happened to her that day. It was as if the weight of the woman's words entered the marrow of her bones, making Delta understand and feel her power as a woman.

She'd thought about that moment many times as a teenager, and when Career Day came in high school, Delta had no doubt what she wanted to hear about.

While her classmates were considering this career or that, they seemed largely undecided about their future.

Not her.

She wanted what that cop had… not the power, but the confidence, the strength, the way she moved in the world, fearless and full of piss and vinegar.

It's amazing how some strangers can impact our world and never know just how much.

Delta's mother had taught her that fear was the most dangerous emotion. Fear kept people from trying new things, from opening their hearts, from tasting everything life had to offer. She told little Delta that people often made poor decisions when fear was involved and advised that she omit it from her emotional repertoire.

Of course, doing so nearly flunked her out of The Academy more than once.

The first time, she and her team were entering a building at night during a simulation, knowing there were perps in it (Sergeants and Captains). When they came to an empty bedroom, she looked in the closet to find the trap door to the attic. She promptly hopped up in there and waited, telling her three male cop teammates to hide. "Let *them* find us. It's better than the other way around. Trust me. They'll never expect it."

They did not listen to her and all three were "killed."

Not her.

No, Delta "Storm" Stevens waited until the "villains" came into the bedroom, irritated they couldn't find her. They were grumbling and bemoaning how long this scenario was taking and of course, it was Storm's team dragging it out.

When they started to leave the room, she dropped down on them, yelled, "Bang! Bang! Bang!" and effectively "killed" all three officer-teachers.

And boy were they pissed.

That was the first time she was called in to discuss the breaking of the rules.

Rules?

"Captain, from what I understand, there are no rules on the street, so why would you employ them here? Aren't these simulations designed to prepare us for real life situations?"

She got off with warning number one.

The second time was when they were learning about car chases. Only in Hollywood do cops use hundred-thousand-dollar vehicles as a barricade. Never in real life. Ever. They are too expensive.

In this simulation, there was a kidnapped child in the escape car.

Delta watched the track carefully, as the first seven cadets failed to catch or stop the vehicle. It was a rigged scenario, to be sure, but what she was able to ascertain was the pattern of the escape vehicle driven by one of the sergeants. When it was her turn, she strapped in, waited for Robyn, the driving instructor to do the same and for the escaping vehicle to take off.

"Go!"

Delta did.

In her mind, she envisioned the pattern of the first seven failures, so when the escape vehicle took a right, she did not.

"What the fuck are you doing?" Robyn, the passenger and driver trainer yelled above the siren.

"Heading them off!"

Delta loved driving the patrol cars, and from the skid pan test to the changing lanes exam, she excelled at them all. The others tried too hard. In their effort to show off their rudimentary high school driving skills, most had failed to recognize the pattern meant to cause a failure.

Not her.

No, she would take an alternate route even though Robyn was yelling something to her about pulling over.

Focused, with her hands lightly gripping the wheel, Delta fishtailed onto a portion of the track no one had gone on yet and floored it.

"What. The. Fuck. Storm?" Robyn yelled as the escape vehicle, once moving away from them was now heading directly toward them about a hundred yards away.

"Stop the fucking car!"

"I've got this, Robyn!" Delta yelled above the siren.

"Stop the motherfucking car!"

Eighty yards.

No one was slowing down.

"Goddamn it!"

Sixty yards.

Delta took her foot off the gas, slammed it on the brake at the same time the Captain did in his car, both turning the car to the left so their driver's side door could be opened upon stopping.

As the two cars skidded to a halt a mere three feet from each other, Delta leapt from the car, pulled her .357 Magnum on the roof, and yelled, "Gotcha!" before the Captain was out of the car.

No one said a word, but the tension was palpable.

The Captain, red-faced, growled, "I'll see both of you in my office," before getting back in the car and driving back to the campus.

"You've done it now," Robyn said, shaking her head as she leaned on the driver's seat to talk to Delta. "You know you can't use the cars as obstructions. You *know* that, Storm. What in the fuck were you thinking?"

Getting back in the car and buckling up, Delta shrugged one shoulder. "I was thinking I wasn't going to fail."

"Oh, you failed all right. The only question remains is whether you just failed this scenario or flunked out of The Academy."

"You *do* know there's usually more than one way to accomplish a task, right? You guys have such a flawed system of right and wrong, black or white, good or bad. That sort of thinking is how cops get killed.

"What I know is there is a right way and you failed to implement it.

"Robyn, there's a right way and a best way, and today, best won."

Robyn shook her head. "Storm, it may have been the best way to beat the scenario, but it was the worst way to embarrass the Captain. You need to be better at picking your battles. I can't help you with this one, so I hope you're prepared for the worst."

Back at the campus, when The Captain finished reaming Robyn for not stopping her, he turned to Delta and spat, "Give me one good reason why I shouldn't kick your ass out of here."

Delta stood tall, her shoulders back, her gaze firmly on him. She thought about her mother's words and reached deep for her courage. "Captain, the day that a car is more valuable than the life of a child is the day I will gladly turn my badge in to become a meter maid."

The others might have failed and perhaps, if this was real life, had consigned a little girl to her death. Or worse.

Not Delta.

Delta Stevens understood what wearing the badge meant. It meant making the hard decisions no one else was willing to make. It meant putting your life on the line for people you didn't know, for people who hated your guts simply because you wore the uniform. She understood the adrenaline rush that came from the danger, as well as the thrill of getting everyone out of a nearly impossible situation in one piece.

Like the one she was currently in.

The call was for a shooter inside a bar. Heavily armed. Better weapons than those they had. He had them all pinned because he possessed an AK, maybe even more than one.

She and her final training partner, Miles Brookman, had been separated upon arrival. Miles had told her to stay with the patrol car while he 'sessed the situation. Most rookies would have gladly remained at a safe distance from this kind of shooting.

Not her.

Once she realized Miles was pinned down, she crept from the patrol car to the utility meter, where she could cover Miles in the event he decided to make a run for it.

This was only their third day on the job together, but already, she liked and respected his work ethic. He was a good guy… a decent human being with a wife and kids he adored. He was also an excellent training patrol teacher who had already taught her so much that The Academy hadn't. She had learned that prostitution was a victimless crime, that burglars who are cornered are more dangerous than robbers who get caught. She'd learned no matter what the lead cop at the scene says, you never, ever put your partner in a vulnerable position, which is why he'd told her to stay in the vehicle. He couldn't look out for both of them until he knew what they were facing.

Right now, they were facing the fact that her partner was in direct line of sight of the shooter, pinned and incapable of making an escape, and it was up to her to get him out of there.

"Miles!" she called out.

When he realized she wasn't in the patrol car, he shook his head. "What the hell are you doing?"

"Giving you some cover! I'll draw his fire!"

"Wait!"

But she did not.

Instead, Delta estimated she was only twenty feet from a big, blue mailbox, which was a safer place for her to be anyway. She was sure she could make it.

Miles rose up, took two shots and watched as the shooter switched from shooting at her to where Miles knelt pinned. She bolted for the mailbox, causing the shooter to swing his rifle back at her and fire three shots into the mailbox.

He may have had a high powered weapon, but his aim was shit.

She took out her .357 and blindly took a shot in order to keep him shooting at her. She was far enough away from Miles now, that he easily got back to the patrol car, where he perched at the wheel hub seconds before the shooter returned his attention to him.

They remained in their positions until the SWAT team arrived and took the guy out with a bullet to the face with *their* rifles. For all the meagre training they received before going on patrol, beast cops had weapons woefully under-powered against gun owners who had military grade weapons.

When they were back in their unit, Miles turned to her. "The next time I tell you to do something, do it."

Delta sighed. "Sorry, Miles. I'm so used to following my own instincts, I failed to respect your experience. It won't happen again."

He looked at her and shook his head. "Of course it will. You just showed me the kind of cop you want to be and it's my job to domesticate your feral ways so you're safe to partner with. Yes, you got me out of a jam. But that could have gone either way."

She nodded. "I guess I'm a shit-doer, Miles. Always have been. You needed to get out of there... I got that shit done. But I hear what you're saying."

His sigh was fueled by frustration. "What is the first thing I told you when you were assigned to me?"

"That our real job was to get home in one piece every night."

"And?"

"And here we are, going home in one piece. Mission accomplished." She forced a smile that was not returned.

Miles chuffed as he shook his head. "You know, they warned me about you."

"They who?"

"*Everyone.*"

"And yet, here I am sitting in a patrol car with you. Why is that?"

He chuckled and shook his head. "I drew the short straw."

A huge grin crept across her face. "Lucky you! I'm a prize, Miles. You'd be lucky to have a partner like me."

"And why is that? You are brash. You don't follow orders. You are apparently fearless, and the word revolving around your name is reckless."

She flashed him a lopsided grin. "I know you don't want to like me, but you do, and you do because I'll do everything in my power to make sure we both get home safely. I was merely doing the job you're teaching me to do."

"Are you being serious right now?"

Delta nodded, her emerald green eyes bemused. "Let me ask you a question. What's the most important thing to you in a friendship?"

Miles cocked his head. "Why?"

"Just answer the question."

He thought for a moment as they pulled into the station. "Trust. If I can't trust you, we have nothing. If we have nothing, we won't make it."

Delta nodded. "Good. Because you can trust me to do *everything* I can to keep us safe and to ensure you go home to your wife and kids. And by everything I mean not even orders will stop that if the orders are incongruous with what I am seeing here with boots on the ground. You ordered me to stay. I did. Then I saw an opportunity to get us both to higher ground, so I took it. Trust me, Miles, I refuse to die out here because we were following orders. Oh no no no."

He shook his head. "I can see you are going to be a handful. What's *your* answer?"

"Loyalty. If you can't be loyal, the truth doesn't matter, your skillset doesn't matter, your courage doesn't matter. If I know you have my back, there's nothing I won't do to win."

Miles shut off the car and turned to her. "I don't get it. Everyone says you're a firebrand, a rebel, a troublemaker, but you seem so…"

"If you say normal, I'm going to punch you in the face."

Miles chuckled. "I was going to say centered."

"Oh. I like that. I accept it. Look, I am very confident in myself, and a confident woman is off-putting to men and women alike. If you're a confident man, people admire you. If you are a confident woman, suddenly you're an arrogant bitch."

"That sounds about right."

"When a woman thinks I am arrogant, it says more about her own teeny tiny self-confidence than it does about me." She shrugged. "I like me. For whatever reason, that bothers all the self-loathers out there. You don't need to *like* me, Miles, but if you don't respect me, please throw me back into the pond and let someone else be my partner who will."

"Whoa. Who said I didn't like you?"

Delta leaned in. "You told me *some* of the things they said about me. What did you leave out?"

Miles cut his eyes away quickly. "Has nothing to do with the job, so it's unimportant."

Delta leaned closer. "Is it? Because it seems to me if you wind up with your training patrol partner, you might want to not only see all of her skeletons, but help her repaint the closet."

He turned back to her. "Your personal life is not germane to our professional partnership."

"That's bullshit, Miles, and you know it. Do you know where my first three training patrol officers took me the first night? All three parked in front of the lesbian bar, *The Driftwood*. Each time I asked what crime is being committed? Nothing. I pointed out that we were wasting taxpayer dollars sitting here visually harassing women who are not breaking any laws. Know what they said?"

Miles shook his head. "No, and I don't want to know. I'm sure it was disgusting and inappropriate."

"To say the least. So I asked two of the other female cadets on training patrol if their trainers took them there. They both looked at me like I was crazy. But I'm not crazy."

"I know that."

"Yeah? Then why do you think I got the *special* treatment of the trip to the lesbian bar?"

"I don't know. I *do* know that some of the other trainers are assholes to the female cops." He turned and stared out the window.

"They are. Do you also know that I'm gay?" She let the word hang in the air as she waited for his reaction.

This wasn't her first rodeo, though she'd had to hide her sexual preference in The Academy. God, how she hated that term. It wasn't a *preference* for her. It had never been a *lifestyle choice*. No second grader makes those decisions, but she'd known then that her crushes were on other girls, and she'd been hiding that fact for years. No one was going to minimize Delta Stevens again or cram her in a box of their own ignorant making. Stonewall had been decades ago, for god's sake.

"Miles? What else did you hear?"

Slowly, he turned back toward her. "I've heard the rumors."

She shook her head. "Rumors like the dyke took out Robert Eli during hand-to-hand because he referred to her as a clit licker? Rumors such as I punched Scott Larson in the Adam's Apple because he tucked a five dollar bill in my belt and asked for a Lesbian Lap Dance? Those rumors?"

"Delta—"

"No, Miles, you need to know the truth. Those aren't rumors. I did all of that, and, quite frankly, a little bit more. I have no regrets. I'll do the same to you or anyone else who tries to belittle me or those I care about simply because of who we choose to love. I'm a fighter, Miles. That's just one reason you should be glad you got me as a rookie, because I won't give up. Ever. I may not always do what's right, but I sure as shit will do what's best. Sometimes, those two things are mutually exclusive."

He stared at her a long time before asking, "Do you play chess?"

She tilted her head at his non sequitur "I know *how*, but I am not any good. Why?" Delta's left eyebrow rose in the shape of a question mark.

"The queen is the most versatile and most powerful of the pieces. It's her versatility that makes her so strong on the chessboard. Conversely, the king can't even get out of his own way. One move here. One move there. Sitting duck for most of the match. I'm no sexist, Delta, but there are times, like today, when I couldn't get out of my own way and I needed your versatility. Was I thrilled I had put us in that position? Of course not. But you found your way around the board and kept me from being pinned down. What I am trying to say here is… I don't give a flying fuck what you do or who you do it with when you are not on duty as long as you keep bringing that sharp attitude and prickly demeanor with you to the job."

Delta leaned back and crossed her arms, a slight grin on her face. "So it's not going to be a problem?"

"I don't know. Is it a problem for you?"

Delta barked a laugh. "Sometimes. Women can be hard."

"Sometimes? Jesus, if *you* can't understand them, what hope is there for the rest of us?"

Delta surprised herself with a belly-laugh as Miles brushed

some shattered glass from the top of the door handle before gripping it. As they started out of the patrol car, they got a call. Miles turned to her and cocked his head. "Well?"

"Hell yeah," she said, buckling back up. "We can write reports later."

Miles grinned as he, too, buckled up and told dispatch they were taking the call. They'd have to head back to the station to deal with the patrol car, but they'd be heading in the right direction anyway, so why not deal with one more call to round off the day?

Delta sighed happily as she stared out the window at the pavements flowing past them on their way.

A lot of other cops would have let it go, preferring to go home, crack open a beer, and leave the dark underbelly of the city for another day.

Not her.

About The Author

Linda Kay Silva (Alex Westmore) was a cop for a second. She was the worst cop in the world. She didn't see the purpose of demeaning people with name-calling. She refused to write 'creative' reports when her partner punched a man in the face whose hands were 'cuffed behind his back. She was heartbroken when they had to take people to the hospital who hadn't needed a hospital *before* law enforcement arrived. In The Academy, she spent most of her time doing push-ups because she often chuckled at the stupid way the drill instructors would scream in their faces over stupid things that didn't matter.

Eventually she moved into education and began to write her series of Delta Stevens novels, starting with *Miles to Go* (originally called 'Taken By Storm'). Delta is the cop LKS would have wanted to be if she'd been able to navigate the sexism, the racism, the bigotry, and the good old boys club.

As one of Linda's most popular series, Delta Stevens, like an oldest child, holds a special place in the heart of the 5 time award winning author of more than 50 novels, which includes the acclaimed *Echo Branson* series.

The Advocate

Clare Stevens

ODAY IS MY birthday. I am ninety. And I'm about to do something I've never done before. I don't know what to wear. It could be cold out there.

I asked my grandson for a strong bicycle D-lock. He raised his eyebrows, but said nothing.

"Are you going to start cycling again Grandma?" said his daughter. She calls me Grandma even though, technically, I'm a Great.

"I'm using it for illicit purposes." I winked at her behind her daddy's back. She's a bright young thing. She'll know what 'illicit' means, and if she doesn't, she can Goggle it.

They named her Elsie after me, because, apparently, she had my eyes when she was a baby. She also has auburn curls, like I did at her age.

Behind my back they call me 'Batty Granny.' They think that I can't hear, but since I've had those new all-singing, all-dancing aids, I hear things I'm not supposed to.

I also need wire cutters, but the lad who comes to do my garden is lending me his. He's a nice young man with a big beard. That seems to be the fashion again. When I told him what I was planning, he didn't bat an eyelid. He just said, "Hey, that's cool," and offered to help.

His name is Jed. I think it's short for Jeremy.

The phone rings, the one with moving pictures on it.

"Happy birthday Grandma!" They sing for me while they're having their breakfast. Mia, the little one, is wearing a pink tutu. It's World Book Day, or something, which means they dress up to go to school. I'm not sure what book she is going as.

As a girl, I used to love dressing up. We had a wooden chest full of costumes. We didn't dress as books though.

"What are you doing for your birthday Grandma?"

"I've got plans for later with my gardener."

After they've gone off to school, I rest. I need to conserve my energy for later. I potter around, make a spot of lunch then nod off for a bit. I'm still nodding when Jed knocks on the door. He's brought the thing he's been constructing for this evening. He's made it out of pallets and bits of off-cut wood. It's a Heath Robinson sort of arrangement involving big strong ropes that he brought from his boat. He lives on a barge down on the canal, apparently.

I'm very light, so this thing should bear my weight. And anyway, at ninety, I'm past caring. If I fall to my death, what a way to go! And what a cause.

People my age, and younger, are worried about falling. Some of them are so frightened they don't leave the house. I've broken almost every bone in my body at some point, probably. But they've managed to put me back together again. And now they have drugs to strengthen our bones, so we no longer look bent over like the figures on the 'old people crossing' road signs you see near care homes.

I've avoided the care homes so far. My family say I stay healthy enough not to need one through sheer stubbornness. But who wants to live with a group of old people who spend all day watching television?

I've packed a little bag. Jed tells me I must take my phone, although I hate being encumbered by the thing. I also take a book. And a torch to read by. I still have some of the big-print books I got from the library before it closed down. They never asked for them back. I mostly have talking books these days, but that might disturb the birds.

We wait till dusk, then make our move. Jed takes me in his van which has a mattress in the back along with his gardening tools because sometimes, when he's not sleeping on his boat, he stays overnight in his van.

When we get to the site, we don't need the wire cutters after all, as Jed spots a gap in the fencing they've put up.

It's dark, but the moon is up, and we're illuminated by its dim light, but inside the fencing, nobody can see us because Jed has put the panels back to hide the gap. He is very efficient.

I'm wearing a kind of fleecy romper suit that my daughter left in the house. It's like a big bear costume with a hood and ears. It's very toasty. Underneath I have lots of layers, because April is the cruellest month. I've also, just in case, worn a pair of those giant pants they gave me at the hospital that time when I had a problem with my waterworks. And earlier I popped one of those bladder control pills alongside my daily cocktail of medication. I don't want to get caught short. There's a portable toilet in the corner of the site, put there for the workmen. I take advantage of it while Jed makes final adjustments to his handiwork. As I battle with the romper suit, I wonder whether wearing it was such a good idea. But needs must!

We pick the biggest tree, the old oak. My favourite. This tree is two hundred and seventy-five years old. Makes me feel like a spring chicken. It's the one we used to climb, as children.

Jed climbs it now to rig up the ropes. He moves with the agility of a monkey.

"I'm so glad young people still climb trees," I tell him.

"Young?" he laughs. "I'm nearly forty!"

Next, he fastens the ropes around the platform he's constructed.

"Will it take my weight?"

"Let's see!" I can tell by the sound of his voice that he's joking.

When I was a little girl, there was a tall sycamore in the field at the back of our house. My brothers made a pulley system which they slung over one of the highest branches. They put me on it to test it out, me being the lightest child, but the rope they used was frayed, and the whole thing started to give about a third of the way up. I plummeted to the ground. I broke my collar bone that time. And my wrist. I had my arm in a sling for weeks. I can see, looking at what Jed has constructed, that this is a far superior system.

These ropes are industrial strength, and the platform is on two levels so I can sit on it, like a sedan chair. That's good because I'm not as flexible as I once was, despite all the yoga.

Before he lifts me on, he records a little video interview with me on his phone.

"Elsie, why are you doing this?"

"Because today is my birthday. I'm ninety years old. And I remember these trees from when I was a little girl. I want them to still be here when I'm a hundred."

He then hoists me up, filming me on his phone as the platform ascends. He climbs the branches again to make sure the construction is solid, wedged in between the biggest boughs. He attaches some more ropes and says, "Good, that's not going anywhere."

After checking I'm ok, he says, "Night Elsie. I'll see you in the morning, and if you need anything, just phone. I'll be sleeping in the van in the street outside. Sweet dreams!"

"Oh, I don't suppose I'll sleep," I say. "But I had a nice long nap in the afternoon, so it doesn't matter."

I sleep more in the daytimes these days anyway.

Jed has spread a quilt from his van out on the platform to keep me cosy. I wrap it round me. It smells of the outdoors and those funny cigarettes people used to smoke in the sixties. I was in my thirties then, and never tried the stuff, but I always liked the smell. It comforts me now to think back…

Although it's night-time, it's not quiet up here among the

treetops. There's an owl somewhere nearby, its toot blending in with the sound of nocturnal motorbikes, circling the town, and the distant hum of traffic.

I don't sleep, but I sink into a reverie, from which I'm roused by the sound of buzzing. I look up, and see it's one of those remote-control helicopter thingies like my grandchildren used to have, before they crashed it. It hovers overhead for a while, and moves off.

Now it's peaceful, until the blackbirds start up, pre-dawn, followed by a robin, a thrush, and more birds, singing their faithful song. I wonder what they think of this strange creature in their midst. I remember the dawn chorus of old. It used to be deafening, each species joining in sequence, like an orchestra. But there are still birds here, for now. They have their hour before the ugly sound of man and machines intrudes.

I want to sit here and enjoy this moment, but my bladder is calling. How annoying! Jed said he'd get me down if I needed the loo but I don't want to disturb him yet. I try to distract myself by identifying bird calls so I can last for another hour or so.

Bladder control is one thing they're keeping an eye on. If I lose it, the dreaded care homes beckon. Waterworks, it seems, are what defines whether you are a responsible adult, capable of living independently, or not.

One of my earliest, most shameful memories is of being at a children's party, aged four, legs crossed, too shy to ask for the lavatory. We stood in a circle to play a game that involved jumping in the air, and I couldn't hold it in any longer. I felt the warm liquid trickle down my leg and tried to pretend the deepening puddle on the floor hadn't come from me. They packed me off home early. They told my parents I'd 'had an accident.' I lived in fear of accidents after that.

Adulthood brings an end to such anxieties, except in dreams, but now, at ninety, my bladder is once more a going concern.

My phone rings. Thinking it's Jed, I pick up, but a woman's voice says: "Is this Elsie Taylor?"

"Who's asking?" I've been told not to get too pally with strangers on the telephone.

"I'm a producer from BBC Radio Nottingham. Is it true you spent the night in a treehouse to protest against planned development?"

"Yes, and I'm still here." To prove it, I hold the phone out to the sounds of birdsong. By now the pigeons have struck up, their brooding chant drowning out the more melodious birds.

"Ok if we do a quick interview on the phone now, and we'll send someone down there?"

Honestly, what a fuss. But fuss is what we need, apparently, to save the trees.

After I do my piece, the phone never stops. After Radio Nottingham, it's Radio Trent, then Radio something else FM. All these radios I didn't know existed. And now the TV want some shots for their breakfast show, or something. Do people really want to look at *me* up a tree while they're eating their breakfast?

Thankfully, I'm having one of my good days, and can find the words to answer all their questions.

The television people arrive, and hot on their heels, that man from the local council. He seems very cross. And there's a man with a fluorescent jacket from the development company too. It sounds like they're having a bit of an argument down there.

But now I really do need the toilet. I'm about to phone Jed when I hear him below, calling up to me. "You ok Elsie?"

"I'm fine, but I need the loo."

He directs while I get into position on the platform and he guides me down. I descend to applause from what is now quite a crowd. And there's a proper cameraman filming my descent. They all want interviews, but I tell them they have to wait, as

Jed leads me to the Portaloo.

"How come all these people are here, Jed?"

"I put that video of you on TikTok. Elsie, you've gone viral."

The TV person points a big fluffy microphone at me.

"What made you become an activist at the age of ninety?"

"I wouldn't describe myself as an activist." I scrabble around in my brain for the word I want.

"I'm more of an advocate. An advocate for the trees!"

✧　　✧　　✧

Today is my birthday. I am ninety-four years old, and it's time for my annual trip to the trees. There is a community here now. They've built little inter-connecting shacks high up in the branches and they have a rota to keep guard. It gives me joy to see these people, mostly at least sixty years younger than me. I'm told one of them's a lawyer and they've found some loophole to stop the developers in their tracks.

I don't stay here at night anymore, my bones and my bladder won't allow it. I just put in a celebrity appearance on my birthday.

I am quoted, and misquoted, in all sorts of places.

Jed is here, with that new mayor woman, who, apparently is on our side. She's put forward some proposal to keep this patch of land as a protected nature reserve in among the planned development. A compromise, but it would mean the trees get to live on. Jed explains all this to me as the woman talks very quickly on her phone.

There are press people here again and I've brought little Elsie, not so little now. In fact, she's taller than me. I let her do the interviews as I'm struggling to find my words nowadays.

"Nature is in massive decline," she tells the crowd, "These trees support entire eco-systems. We need to preserve habitats like this, not destroy them."

I'm glad the focus is on her because it means I'm invisible so nobody will notice that I'm crossing my legs like a child.

The mayor woman comes off her phone and steps forward. She announces something I can't quite catch, and a huge cheer goes out.

And now, the cameras all pan around to me, and the reporters crowd around. They ask me what I think about what the mayor's just said.

"Elsie, how does it feel to know you've won?"

I don't understand what anyone's saying and I can't find my words. All I can think about is the trickle of warm liquid now running down the inside of my trouser leg.

Little Elsie steps forward, hugs me and becomes my voice.

"My great grandma is a living legend," she says. "I'm so proud of her. This amazing news that the trees are now safe is all down to her. She's a massive role model for people my age and the perfect advocate for the planet."

The ground is wet from overnight rain, so one more puddle won't make much difference. It's not important, anyway. We're here for the trees. And apparently, we've won!

I smile for the cameras, as the crowd breaks into a chorus of 'Happy Birthday'.

About The Author

Clare grew up in the wilds of Somerset where a daily diet of ghost stories cooked up in her older sister's imagination fostered a love of storytelling long before she could read or write. She has lived most of her adult life in Nottingham.

She began her career as a journalist, before spending several years in government communications. She later embarked on an MA in Creative Writing, which she passed with distinction. Clare wrote her first novel *Blue Tide Rising* (Inspired Quill, 2019) while on the course. Her second novel, *Heartsound*, was published in 2023.

She's featured in John Baird's book *Follow the Moon and Stars, a literary journey through Nottinghamshire,* (Five Leaves Publications, 2022) alongside literary greats like Lawrence and Byron, and contemporary Notts authors.

Clare's favourite writing time is first thing in the morning when she's still half in dreamland. She also writes in cafes and other public spaces, drawing inspiration from the unlimited supply of human interest.

Ones At The Edge

E.J. Runyon

GORDO DROVE RATHER sanely for a guy with a full-sized mattress set strapped onto his '71 Impala's roof. The rising sun struck his rear-view mirror at an annoying angle, but he was patient. It would move. With an open can of Coors sweating between his legs, four more cans cooling his ankles and his cousin's truant wife, Bernie, silent and still next to him, he steered westward.

Bernie hadn't exactly told her husband Carlos why she was going. She didn't need to. In the counselor's office she'd only straightened her shoulders and, keeping her hands down in her lap, she'd said, "I can go for good, or if you'd rather, I can go for the summer. What's better for you?" It seemed easier on him that way.

She'd stared at Carlos' knees, because her eyes wouldn't move any higher, holding herself tight the way she did. If she unfocused her eyes the carpet did a neat switch of perception, the beige parts becoming borders for the green areas. She waited for his answer, concentrating on the squares of carpet. Never stronger than at that moment. Never surer she'd be dead by the time he pulled the truck into their driveway. But taking that deep breath and saying it out loud just the same.

✧　✧　✧

THE BEADS OF her rosary slipping though Bernie's fingers in clicks were the only sound in the car. "Please, don't turn it on, okay?" she whispered when Gordo reached for the radio. She wanted what she wanted, so now Gordo found he felt antsier in the quiet than he'd expected to. But that was okay too.

She fingered the beads one by one. *The moment I moved out.* Repeated in her mind, with each click. *This day. I moved out.* The sunrise hadn't fully breached the horizon behind her yet. The quiet felt good. She loved the colors rising slowly around her.

The next bead brought a vision of herself just minutes ago, in her driveway, the still cool air against her neck. Taking one last look before getting into Gordo's car. Her forehead between her brows wrinkled into those two little up and down lines that Carlos liked about her. Her shoulders tensed as she ticked the items off on her thin fingers, squinting up into the dimness of the early morning hour. Carlos was not due home from his graveyard shift at the bottling plant for a while.

Bernie was still in a hurry to get going out of the driveway.

Another bead clicked and she heard his voice: "I'll give you a check." Carlos had told her, "You give that to the guy and be sure you get a receipt. Don't let him say in month two that he needs any more. Got it?"

He'd sat on the edge of their bed watching her pull a small handful of underwear from the laundry basket, to add to her stack of summer clothes from the drawers of her bureau.

"I won't, Carlos."

"Better not."

The beads slipped through Bernie's fingers like holy water in a font. Gordo remained tranquil in the face of no music, one hand high on the wheel, glad there weren't tears to deal with, no tirades. Until Bernie let out that sound. A stifled whimper.

He felt its push, like a live thing. Getting under his sternum, the sensation ran down his arms to his fingertips, like his Impala shuddering and slipping out of gear that winter when his transmission was all jacked up.

Gordo glanced in every one of his rear-view mirrors before tucking his chin down for another sip of beer. He stared straight ahead. "You need somebody, you call me. Okay?"

After killing the first beer Gordo made a bold decision and a wide detour. He exited the freeway and headed up to an IHOP. North, up a ways on Figueroa, stopping because he said they needed gas. But it was really to get some food into her. She was way too thin. Had to turn sideways twice just to cast a shadow. Girls needed a bit of meat on them. Pancakes, Gordo thought. Yeah, that's what she needs.

Bernie sat, hunched. Her short stack missing only a few token bites; for Gordo's benefit. Her wedding ring clinked once against her cup, louder in the empty seating section than it should have sounded. She looked at her hand like she'd just found it there on the table, a tip from the last customer. Nothing to do with her order at all. She slipped the ring off and into the pouch of her black hoodie. Then she started talking. Softly.

Bernie didn't consider herself a fugitive wife for two reasons: she touched the tip of her ring finger with her thumb, explaining to Gordo: "One. Carlos agreed to let me take the three months' rent plus deposit from his account."

She held onto that reason the tightest. Seeing Carlos' face as she looked off past Gordo's shoulder, "You're gonna need it. Don't tell me no, Bernie."

She didn't want to take anything from him that she'd have to come back and give him later. But Bernie kept that to herself.

The passing waitress broke her view of their bedroom and Bernie blinked, focusing on Gordo again. Her thumb to her middle finger now. Tapping this one, like it meant more.

"And two, you're a valid witness, Gordo. You saw what I've brought. Only the brass bed, my rocking chair, two boxes of books and my summer clothes."

Gordo nodded okay. "Sure." Wishing he had his beer under the table there. He added, "Hey, Bern, eat something, will ya? One more bite at least." Pushing her plate closer to her elbow. What else could he do? He could dawdle over a carafe of stale coffee, hoping she'd change her mind and ask to be taken back home, but in the end he saw; it was her story, she was sticking to it. They got back on the road.

Bernie had asked for the ride. And that's all Gordo was doing here. Giving the girl a ride.

✧   ✧   ✧

"HEY, BABE," CARLOS had reached for her there in the bedroom, and pulled her to the bed, setting her between his knees and leaning his forehead on her middle, tender like he used to. "Just remember, you let me live like a bachelor, no telling how the house'll look come September." He smiled up at her and put his chin on her bellybutton, wiggling his eyebrows to make her laugh. Carlos; the good guy in this all of a sudden.

She tried not to pull away, tried to pay attention through her skin to all the things he was working to get across. But it was too late; she couldn't feel a thing.

Finally, there in the counselor's office, Carlos had answered: low, tired, no more patient breaths in and out. Giving in; "Three months, Bernie. No more. More- I- I couldn't take no more."

And the only thing keeping her from saying who'd had to take what so far was the ache in her wrist and the memory of coming to with her head up against the tile of the bathroom, where he'd slammed her that last time.

✧   ✧   ✧

AT THE PATIO dinners the family had whispered about why they thought she was going, of what Carlos thought about it – just never talking in front of Bernie. Gordo ignored all the questions his side of the family burned to ask. Knowing they'd never ask Bernie directly. "You find out what the hell Bernadette's gonna do all by herself in the damn Hollywood," his aunt Arlene, Carlos' mother, pushed at the last get-together. "Is it a fella?" Gordo's dad whispered; his can of beer shaking in his palsied hand. "She likes you, Gordo, you find out, mi hijo."

"Nah, Linda. It can't be no man." Nadine was sure. The younger cousins, both girls, shook their heads over their plates of pollo asado. Babies on their laps, the two girls leaned in, eyes shining, like watching a novela on TV in the kitchen. Ignoring the shouts from their kids running through the sprinklers on the side of the lawn. "With Carlos? C'mon. This nice place? What more could she want?"

In the kitchen, Bernie's Aunt Maria had shaken her hand at her. "Here." Palm down and curled around something. "Quiet," she added, because the door was open to the backyard, the bougainvillea shining bright magenta in the sun. Green plastic chairs scattered under the jacaranda trees and the littlest kids running everywhere and screeching.

Bernie looked down at four folded one hundred dollar bills, unfurling in Maria's now up-turned hand like a green bud opening, then back up at Maria. Maria shoved them at her, "Go on." Then she picked up the biggest platter of tacos and bumped closed an open drawer with her hip as she walked out to the others, "Linda," she called, "get the sour cream, Chula, I got too much in my hands."

"Father Rudolph must be rolling over right now, mama," Nadine had joked. The women unconsciously hugged their purses closer to their sides as the three of them walked up the drive towards the bright red of the psychic's front door. Bernie never carried a purse; she had no car keys, and Carlos only gave her the money she needed for the exact errand she was allowed to go on.

"Father Rudolph's not the boss of me." Maria reached to the center of the red door and knocked.

Mrs. Ileana gave Bernie a look when she took hold of her hand, running her fingers over some of the lines on Bernie's open palm.

The three women sat and watched in the normal looking dining room (except for that money slot), and Bernie, nervous, made a closer survey of the woman now holding her hand.

She wore a woven jet black shawl; the coarse weave was shot through with iridescent threads – like she was wrapped in a starry night.

Bernie's hand trembled when the psychic shook her head, glancing quickly at Maria. Bernie was sure she knew all about the concussion and her wrist.

The psychic's tone was confident, "You're a person who'll gravitate toward the ones at the edge. The loners. The outcasts. But at your own detriment. Your own life will be in danger of going unrecognized." Nadine made a clicking noise with her tongue. Detriment, she'd said; was that Carlos?

With all the lamps so bright in the psychic's living room, that wasn't the spooky part. Leaning in to see where her life was slipping away to, Bernie felt the pain rise up and leave her wrist, like naming the problem had relieved the ache. That was the spooky part.

Later, when they were out driving, Bernie tried to explain what it was like to Carlos, about how bright that red door was and how the spookiness felt, about the beautiful shawl. Not her nodding in agreement, not the pain miraculously lifting; "Gravitate," Carlos mimicked, and changed lanes too roughly, with quick jerks of the wheel.

Bernie, so lightweight, slid away from him on the truck's bench seat from his swerving. She was glad she hadn't thought of adding empathetic too, (the other thing the psychic had told her). Bernie's sore shoulder banged against the passenger's door before she could reach out to Carlos to stop herself from falling away from him.

✧   ✧   ✧

THE APARTMENT HOUSE she found was a three-story brick building that sat about six yards up from the edge of the Hollywood Freeway, just off the northbound Sunset exit. At the bottom end of a cul-de-sac, up against the constant rush of traffic sounds, where Antoinette Place and Lorenzo Way met. It was a fluke that she'd found it at all. Carlos had gone fishing up at the Santa Fe Dam with his papi and his tío Raul and Bernie had the rare weekend to herself.

Nadine's call came practically before Carlos's truck had cleared their driveway. "Hey, chica, your mama says you're free this weekend, let's go get crazy while you got a chance."

Bernie liked Nadine, maybe more than any of the other cousins she'd married into. She always talked way tougher than she was. "Okay," Bernie agreed, "What's your preference?"

"For crazy there's only one place, baby." So they ended up taking Nadine's two boys and driving into Hollywood, first going up into Griffith Park with a picnic. Nadine's idea of crazy was anything that got her and the kids out of her own place. She liked the green. And she liked driving to find it. The apartment Luis had for them squatted, surrounded in browns, grays and tans, with mostly dirt out front and parking in the back. Right up next to the next apartment on the block was more dirt and more parking, and the next and the next.

"Man, this is the life, huh?" Nadine leaned back on her elbows on the quilt Bernie had thought to bring with them. Nadine stroked the black brush-cut hair of her youngest, Raymond. The seven-year-old laid in a C-shape next to his mom, his back to her thighs, shoes pulled off, toes in the grass, smiling, full of egg sandwiches, peaches and Fritos, almost asleep. Gilbert, Nadine's other one, was off sword fighting a tree with a branch he'd stripped from some bush along the path. It had been a walk to get to the picnic area from where they'd left the car.

"This is way better than the recreation center. This is nearly as good as your backyard."

Bernie shielded her eyes, watching Gilbert attack the trees, resigned to the fact that this was as crazy as it got.

Later, Nadine headed down Western to Hollywood Boulevard, searching for even more variations of green. But she promised them Slurpies for good behavior on the drive back. So then Nadine and Bernie took their time strolling up and down some of the streets looking at the cool apartments in the little neighborhoods off of Wilton Place; bird-of-paradise flowers in nearly every yard. Lantana bushes spilling onto the sidewalks in knee-high humps of purples and yellows, occasionally a dividing hedge in a burnt orange color. Roses.

No Jacaranda trees, like in Bernie's backyard, but lots to see all the same. The architecture appealed to Bernie more than Nadine's need for green.

"It's like being back in the Forties," Bernie said.

"If you say so. You're the reader."

"I'm the reader too," Raymond piped in. And in a flash Bernie realized that she'd be going. Raymond, tugging at Bernie's hand as they walked, asked, "What 'chu gonna do for the summer, Aunt Bernadette?"

She spun him in a circle in front of her, like a dance move, "What're you gonna do?" Nadine corrected.

"I'm gonna be in second when school goes again. I'm gonna be a reader too," Raymond tugged for another spin.

Bernie looked up into the trees, "I could use a break."

"Who can't?" Nadine said, "Gilbert Rios, you tear one more flower off one more bush and, mi hijo, you're gonna get it."

That's when they came to the apartment. Bernie just knew.

There was a red and white FOR RENT sign in one of the lower windows and Bernie quickly spun Raymond around to face the other way. Away from the building. Suddenly superstitious. As if no one saw her interested, it might end up being hers. "Let's try this street."

She looked for a bus line as they walked back to Nadine's car and memorized its number. She came back that following day.

✧　✧　✧

AS GORDO TURNED off Hollywood Boulevard onto her new street Bernie saw the loveseat and chair set in the corner storefront of a cheap furniture place, a big sign in faded red and blue on the window read: $259.95/SET

"Stop! That's it. I've been looking for that." Gordo swerved into the parking lot without a question and ten minutes later they'd arranged to pick up the two pieces after they'd gotten the mattress set unloaded. The stuff looked like play furniture to Gordo. But he wasn't the one who bought it.

Gordo didn't ask "Why do you need a new loveseat? You've got a living room full of stuff at home." And Bernie never made full eye contact in case he might.

✧　✧　✧

"THE WROUGHT IRON on the back window's come loose," she'd told Carlos, setting a plate of fried potatoes and eggs down in front of him, using her good wrist with the heaped plate. It was a week before Gordo promised to drive her, "I was out in the yard. The stucco, it's crumbling around the bolts."

"Yeah."

Just yeah. Not a mean yeah, an empty one. No cross-examination on how the hell would she know iron from stucco, crumbly or not? No grumbling or tossing his beer can extra hard into the sink to make her jump, no laughing at her words or complaining, "Shit, Bernie, what else?"

Just – yeah.

And now Gordo was saying she could call him if she needed to. Was the world gonna end next?

And now here she was. Moving in. A neighbor holding the building's glass doors wide for her and Gordo. The tall girl smiled. "Here you go," she said in a deep, smoky voice, then followed them in. She looked like she'd been out for an early morning stroll. Bernie's smile just grew and grew. Strolling.

✧ ✧ ✧

THE NEIGHBOR ASKED, "What floor?" after Bernie introduced herself. And Bernie's smile just got wider and wider as it dawned on her. Here was this slim, nicely made-up girl/guy, in a pretty velour jogging suit. Wearing earrings even. Curly hair in a tidy cut: professional, looking down at Gordo and Bernie from about three inches above the top of Gordo's head. Her hands wide – no – wider than Carlos' or even his dad's. And a voice like a well, but with, what? A softness under the words? Sadness?

Bernie couldn't keep the bubbles of happy in her contained. Just being so near. She stuffed her rosary in her jeans and squeezed into the narrow elevator, next to the sideways loveseat, the last of her boxes and the two full pillowcases. "Three."

She beamed, not caring if she was talking to a her or a him.

Bernie's forehead itched, but the little loveseat pinned her, so she shook her head, pony-like and puffed a breath up at her forehead. They caught each other's eye. And the guy/girl grinned at her. Bernie thought, this is some new kind of freedom. Here was someone from her own tribe, a tribe she'd only just realized existed. The strollers of the world. The readers.

Gordo sneezed. And for a second Bernie remembered who she was supposed to be.

✧ ✧ ✧

STANDING ALONE NOW that Gordo had gone, she pulled her wedding ring from the hoodie's pouch. *Why didn't I bring a radio or tape player?* The silence around her felt like too much space in her head. She wasn't sure where to set her ring. It wasn't a safe silence like in Gordo's car. Maybe because here in this room everything was still, nothing rushing by on the periphery. The bumpy pale ceiling seemed too far away.

Bernie stepped into the little dressing room, slipped her ring into one of the big drawers, and heard the clunks it made as it rolled. She thought about setting up a pallet, from clothes and blankets, and sleeping in this small space, instead of in that big space out there. Too big for just her alone yet. That new big space left room for thoughts like: Why are you doing this?

The new carpet smell and the bare, cream-colored walls added to her sense of feeling detached, floating. And no matter how much Bernie's mind kept repeating, *What now Bernadette?* she couldn't be sure why she even kept asking.

While Gordo had been there helping, he'd gotten to work by pulling a screwdriver and a baggie full of bolts from his cargo pants and set up her bed frame and mattresses. He pushed it back against the wall, there in the corner away from the windows. "Nah, let's put it under the window." Bernie asked, "Can we?"

"There's no bars here, Bernadette," was all he said when she pointed to the other side of the wide room.

"Gordo, we're on the third floor." Bernie walked out pacing from wall to wall, front door to windows, head down,

171

counting until she reached fifteen. Just like Carlos, she thought, always for my own benefit. Yet never what I ask for. Then she galloped across the room and, from the breakfast nook, paced to the closet alcove; twenty.

Three windows faced north. Her view, once she stopped with her pacing, stunned her into stillness. The hills rose and ribboned with pastel houses that peeked from the green in the distance. "Third floor's good," Gordo said, ignoring her stillness next to him.

She backed away from the window to get all three of the panes all in one view. "A panorama," Bernie whispered.

Gordo, standing silhouetted in the frame of the window's light, hands on hips, just like Carlos always stood, ignored that too. "No freeway noise," he said. "You're gonna need food, Bernie." He bent for the screwdriver there on the beige carpet and straightened, stiff. First he reached into his pocket for the last can of Coors, then dug in another for his car keys. He popped the can and sipped, stepping back to the view and leaning to inspect the no-bars situation. "Lemme drive you now. You won't have to walk with bags," he told the windows.

"Sit." She patted the new loveseat. "Take a moment and drink your beer. Rest a bit, Gordo." Carlos hated any furniture with a pattern to the fabric, flowered prints especially, which was why she'd only taken her rocking chair, nothing else was worth sitting on. If Gordo tried sitting on this little thing his legs and knees would stick out. And Carlos was no taller than Gordo.

The new little loveseat's fabric, brushed cotton, looked like a metal-flake tan of a new truck, birds with wings wide flew and perched on Japanese-looking tree branches. The branches were loaded with mauve buds and flowers, like a watercolor scene, with shades of grays and blues.

Gordo looked at the loveseat, "I'm okay." He continued his patrolling of the room's perimeter.

"You need a chain for that door." He knocked his knuckle

on the wall over her headboard. He flipped the switch in the tiny walk-in alcove, opening the built-in drawers and sticking his head in the bathroom. "Light's out in here. Get bulbs too. Or borrow one from that freak."

Meg. Bernie remembered her name. She ignored Gordo and his prowling, remained at the loveseat, stroking the satiny feel of the fabric, mentally planning how to rearrange the set around her rocking chair once he left.

She looked at the clock. He'd been home already now for five hours and eighteen minutes.

The little blue alarm clock Gordo had set up on an empty box next to the bed, for a nightstand, ticked and ticked.

The whole house would have been cleaned by noon, and on the days he worked his double shifts Bernie would only be there waiting for the moment to exchange the TV's noise for the sound of his truck pulling back out of the garage at 2 o'clock. Waiting so she could set herself in neutral until he came back. "Please God," she prayed out loud, in the middle of so little, "now that I've left him, let me be something grander than just that girl."

She yanked again and now the box spring slid off the frame and onto the carpet. She propped the top mattress on its side against the wall and bent to tackle the heavier piece next.

About The Author

E.J. Runyon lives in the US North East. Since 2002 she's found herself moving on to smaller and smaller towns, while working to become the author and writing coach she planned on being.

First, she quit working in software and sold her home to finance her degree in Creative Writing and her Grad-work in Online Teaching and Learning. She's never looked back. Now, her life revolves around her own writing and her online creativity coaching business she runs and, you know, being a better person day to day.

Her debut novel for Inspired Quill, *A House of Light & Stone*, was nominated for the 2015 Dramatic Fiction award at The Golden Crown Literary Society (GCLS). Other titles from Inspired Quill include *Claiming One (2012)*, *Tell Me How To Write A Story (2013) and 900 Miles (2020)*. And from other presses: *Your Little Red Book*, *Good People* and *5 Ways of Thinking to Turn Your Writing World Around*.

Dear Reader

Thank you for reading *Root Cause: A Collection of Stories on Community*. If you enjoyed this book (or even if you didn't) please consider leaving a star rating or review online. Your feedback is important, and will help other readers to find the book and decide whether to read it, too.

Acknowledgements

Despite running a publishing house for almost fifteen years, I've never had to write an Acknowledgements Page before. (Dear IQ authors, this is tougher than I've ever given it credit for – I understand now!)

This is also the first time that we've attempted to produce a collection with work from different authors. When I first floated the idea of a collection on the theme of community, with proceeds being split between grassroots nonprofits and mutual aid funds, the positive response made me exceedingly proud to be surrounded by so many wonderful human beings in an industry that can – at times – feel a bit like walking through the swamp of sadness.

To that end, I would like to sincerely thank the IQ authors for their patience while I figured out the three-hundred-and-six moving parts to this project; the emails back and forth; the hastily-scribbled updates in between other projects; and the kindness and energy that kept me going to see this through. Special thanks to Clare Stevens for the impeccably swift proof edit. Hopefully our teamwork pays off and will be reflected in the donations we'll get to send out.

Massive appreciation also goes to the wonderful Martina Pellecchia for the amazing and eye-catching cover. Your patience and artistic eye throughout the whole (lengthier-than-anticipated!) process gave the book's visual element an even keel that was sorely needed. And to produce such a masterpiece in our very first project together bodes (I hope) incredibly well for long, fruitful collaboration. (I promise not to spend so long between feedback next time!)

Evan, (better known as EA Mylonas), our catch-up meetings and your uncanny ability to understand anything I delegate within about 4.2 seconds means this project could be completed (mostly) on time, and to budget. You have been a pleasure to work with, and I hope that our next anthology (spoiler alert!) will keep our wheels turning in the same direction – forward!

Finally, (and most cliché) thank you to our readers. For those of you now reading this particular title, of course, but also to everyone who has supported IQ over the years to make this project possible in the first place.

By purchasing this (and other titles), you're helping to make the world a better place.

List of Contributors

(by order of appearance)

Additional works listed below are Inspired Quill standalone titles or series. All are available from the Inspired Quill website. (www.inspired-quill.com/books)

Anne Goodwin (The Witch's Funeral):
Sugar and Snails, Becoming Someone, Underneath, Matilda Windsor Is Coming Home.

Craig Hallam (Tending Hope):
Greaveburn, Alan Shaw Trilogy (The Adventures of Alan Shaw, Old Haunts, Grave Purpose), Oshibana Complex, Down Days.

James Webster (Seeing The Stars):
Heroine Chic, Monstrous Ink, Hopefully Ever After.

Dorothy A. Winsor (Home):
The Wind Reader, The Wysman, The Trickster, Glass Girl, Dragoncraft.

Howard Robinson (There But For The Grace of God):
Micah Seven Five, Know Your Own Darkness.

David Wilkinson (Liminal Voyage):
We Bleed The Same, Under The Shell.

Daniel Stride (Seven Days to Save Bakatam):
Old Phuul.

EA Mylonas (The One Who Bears A Tree Upon Her Back):
The Hush.

Hugo Jackson (Villainous):
The Resonance Tetralogy (Legacy, Fracture, Ruin's Dawn, Edge of Ascension), Remnant's Hope.

Alex Westmore (Not Her):
Echo Branson Investigations (Before The Echo, Shattered Echo, Echo Returns & more to come), Delta Stevens Crime Logs (Miles To Go, Con Game, Not In The Cards, Taylor Made & more to come).

Clare Stevens (The Advocate):
Blue Tide Rising, Heartsound.

E.J. Runyon (The Ones At The Edge):
Claiming One, A House of Light and Stone, 900 Miles, Tell Me How To Write A Story.

www.ingramcontent.com/pod-product-compliance
Lightning Source LLC
Chambersburg PA
CBHW032008180726
48283CB00008B/2586